"You're a hero."

"Stop saying that. I'm
didn't do anything t
department wouldn'

"But they didn't step in front of that bullet," Erin said. "You did."

"It was reflex, nothing more."

"Why won't you take credit for it? Why didn't you tell me about it?"

He arched his brows. "Would you have believed me?"

"Probably not. I would have figured you'd made it up to impress me, to get me to change my mind about you."

"So why do you believe it now?"

Dear Reader,

I think it's important that we all have a hero—someone we aspire to be like or someone who inspires us to be more than we are or someone who takes care of us. When I was growing up, my big brother was my hero. He defended me against the neighborhood bully and piggybacked me across the creek because I couldn't swim. Heroes also protect us—like the heroes in my CITIZEN'S POLICE ACADEMY series.

Writing *Once a Hero,* the second book in the miniseries (the first was also part of the MEN MADE IN AMERICA miniseries—*Once a Lawman,* HAR, Feb. 2009), was very important to me. Sergeant Kent Terlecki is a hero whose story needed to be told even though he's uncomfortable with being called that. He doesn't consider himself to be special, and neither does heroine Erin Powell. Well, not at first!

I hope you enjoy their story, in which they both learn *Once a Hero,* always a hero.

Happy reading!

Lisa Childs

Once a Hero

LISA CHILDS

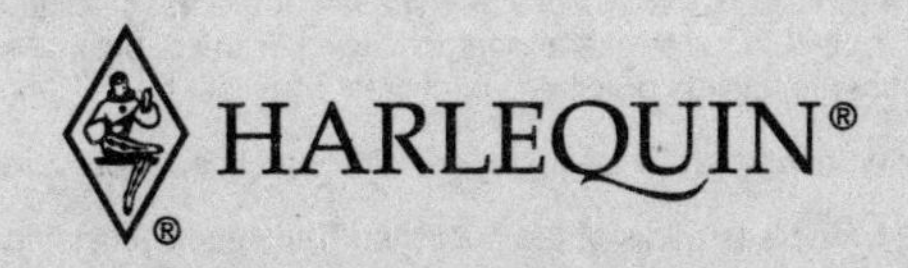

TORONTO • NEW YORK • LONDON
AMSTERDAM • PARIS • SYDNEY • HAMBURG
STOCKHOLM • ATHENS • TOKYO • MILAN • MADRID
PRAGUE • WARSAW • BUDAPEST • AUCKLAND

Recycling programs
for this product may
not exist in your area.

ISBN-13: 978-0-373-75262-1
ISBN-10: 0-373-75262-8

ONCE A HERO

This edition published by arrangement with Harlequin Books S.A.

www.eHarlequin.com

Printed in U.S.A.

ABOUT THE AUTHOR

Bestselling, award-winning author Lisa Childs writes paranormal and contemporary romance for Harlequin/Silhouette Books. She lives on thirty acres in west Michigan with her husband, two daughters, a talkative Siamese and a long-haired Chihuahua who thinks she's a rottweiler. Lisa loves hearing from readers, who can contact her through her Web site, www.lisachilds.com, or by snail mail at P.O. Box 139, Marne, MI 49435.

Books by Lisa Childs

HARLEQUIN AMERICAN ROMANCE

1198—UNEXPECTED BRIDE*
1210—THE BEST MAN'S BRIDE*
1222—FOREVER HIS BRIDE*
1230—FINALLY A BRIDE*
1245—ONCE A LAWMAN†

HARLEQUIN NEXT

TAKING BACK MARY ELLEN BLACK
LEARNING TO HULA
CHRISTMAS PRESENCE
"Secret Santa"

HARLEQUIN INTRIGUE

664—RETURN OF THE LAWMAN
720—SARAH'S SECRETS
758—BRIDAL RECONNAISSANCE
834—THE SUBSTITUTE SISTER

*The Wedding Party
†Citizen's Police Academy

With much gratitude to the
Grand Rapids Police Department for helping me
understand and appreciate the very special heroes
that police officers are.

And with love for my brothers,
Tony, Mike and Chris—for showing me my
first examples of heroism by being my heroes!

Chapter One

Conversations stopped and heads swiveled toward her as Erin Powell walked into the meeting room on the third floor of the Lakewood Police Department. Since she was the first *citizen* to arrive for the Citizen's Police Academy program, the people staring at her were men and women "in blue." The Lakewood, Michigan, police department, however, wore black uniforms, which she believed matched one particular officer's soul.

Despite all the stares, her gaze was drawn to *his*. Sergeant Kent Terlecki's steely-gray eyes must have been how he'd earned his nickname Bullet. She had asked the blond-haired man a couple of times for an explanation of his moniker, but he had shrugged off that question, just as he'd shrugged off most of her others. Some public information officer he'd proved to be for the department—a media liaison who wouldn't deal with the media.

Ignoring the unwelcoming looks and the awkward silence, Erin squared her shoulders and walked across the room toward where all the officers stood against the far wall. She dropped her organizer onto a table, the thud echoing in the large space.

As if he intended to cite her for disturbing the peace, Terlecki stalked over to her. His long-legged strides closed the distance between them in short order.

"Speak of the devil," she murmured.

"I'm not, but that doesn't stop you from demonizing me," he accused as he held out a folded section of the *Lakewood Chronicle.*

Satisfaction filled her as she stared down at the article she had written—about *him*. She wanted everyone to see Kent Terlecki as the fraud he really was, and so she had titled her article, *Public Information Officer's Desperate PR Ploy.*

"Did I hit a nerve?" she asked, tipping up her chin to meet that hard gaze of his. While she was above average height, he was taller, with broad shoulders. But he didn't intimidate her, although she suspected he tried.

"You'd have to actually write a grain of truth to hit a nerve, so I don't think there's any chance that you'll ever do that, Ms. Powell."

Ignoring the sting of his insult, Erin smiled and asked, "If you think I'm such a hack, why did you let me into the class?"

The paper rustled as he clenched his hand into a fist. "Despite what your article claims, I'm not in charge of the Citizen's Police Academy—not as a desperate maneuver to improve the department's image or my own. Neither needs improving."

"Really?" She lifted a brow skeptically. "According to the last poll in the *Chronicle,* the public believes the Lakewood PD could use some improvement."

"That poll was hardly fair," he griped. "There was no option for 'no improvement necessary.'"

"Of course *you* would think no improvement was necessary."

He lifted the paper. "Instead of writing about me, you should have written about the true purpose of this program."

"And what is that?" Although she had signed up to participate, she wasn't entirely certain what the academy did offer.

"Watch Commander Lieutenant Patrick O'Donnell started the program three years ago so that interested members of the community could learn more about the department, about police procedure and about the challenges officers face while doing their job."

His words grated her nerves. Whenever Terlecki actually deigned to speak, it was always in the form of a press release. To irritate him, she arched a brow and scoffed, "*You* have challenges?"

He sighed. "I have *you*, Ms. Powell."

"Oh, so if it was up to you, I wouldn't be here." She had already guessed as much.

The sergeant planted his palms on the table between them and leaned forward until his face nearly touched hers. With his square jaw clenched, he lowered his voice and murmured, "If it was up to me..."

Erin drew in a shaky breath and braced herself as a rush of adrenaline quickened her pulse and warmed her skin. It had to be adrenaline; she could not be attracted to *this* man.

"If it was up to you?" she pressed.

His pupils widened until black swallowed the gray irises. "I'd—"

"I hope I didn't miss anything," a woman interrupted as she rushed up to join them.

Sergeant Terlecki stepped back. "Not at all. Class hasn't started yet," he assured her, before turning and walking back to his fellow officers.

Erin released the breath she'd been holding, as the other woman emitted a lusty sigh.

"Oh, I think I did miss something," the newcomer insisted, staring after Terlecki.

Erin pushed her organizer farther down the table and settled onto a chair away from the younger woman. Erin was the one who'd missed something—hearing about whatever Sergeant Kent Terlecki wanted to do to her. But given the articles she wrote about how inept he was at his job, at keeping the public informed, she could guess....

HE WANTED TO WRING her pretty little neck. Kent relaxed his fingers, which had clutched the *Chronicle* so tightly the newsprint had torn. He tossed it on the table behind which most of the officers were talking amongst themselves, as the citizens filed in for class.

The watch commander, Lieutenant Patrick O'Donnell, glanced up from marking notes on index cards. "So what's her deal with you?" he asked, nodding toward Erin Powell. "Did you break her heart?"

Kent snorted. "I doubt she actually has a heart. Or a soul."

Paddy, as he was called by his friends, chuckled. "How do you *really* feel about her?"

Kent wished he knew. She was so damn infuriating, yet she fascinated him, too. "I think I need my head examined for agreeing to let her join the academy."

Paddy narrowed his eyes, which were nearly the same reddish brown color of his hair, and scrutinized Kent. "I left it up to you. I would have been happy to decline her application."

Paddy had begun the Lakewood Citizen's Police Academy before he'd been promoted to watch commander, but even after his promotion, he continued as lead instructor. The program was his pet project and meant a lot to the lieutenant.

"I'm sorry about her article," Kent murmured.

Paddy shrugged. "Why? You can't control what she writes."

No, he couldn't, despite his best efforts. She always found something wrong with his press releases about accidents or shootings. She always accused him of hiding something from the public no matter how open he was with information. "She didn't give you the credit you deserve."

The lieutenant chuckled again. "I'm perfectly happy with her *not* writing about me."

"That's why I okayed her joining," Kent admitted. "I'd hate to think what she would have written if you'd turned down her application." Chances are she would have accused them of conspiring against her.

He glanced over, to find her scribbling something on her ever-present pad. Since class hadn't started yet, he doubted she was jotting down notes on the CPA. She was probably working on another article about how incompetent he was in his undeserved position.

A lock of silky brown hair slid across her cheek until she pushed it behind her ear. Her eyes were the same chocolate-brown. And her figure…it was tall and slender, with curves in all the right places. How could she be so damn pretty, yet such a witch?

"I'm really not worried about her writing about me," Paddy assured him. "She seems pretty focused on *you*."

"Too focused." Since Erin had been hired at the *Chronicle* a year ago, Kent had often been the subject of her articles. She was young, ambitious and obviously trying to make a name for herself, so he tried not to take it personally, but he couldn't help thinking that it *was* personal.

Again he looked toward the table where she sat. While the young girl who'd interrupted them waved, Erin glared at him. "I don't know what I could have done to her," he murmured.

Paddy followed his gaze. "You're sure you didn't break her heart?"

Kent shook his head. He would have remembered if he'd ever dated Erin Powell. Her dark hair skimmed the edge of her delicate jaw, emphasizing those wide brown eyes and sharp cheekbones. She was really beautiful, but he'd rather date one of the K9s than her. The police dogs were less likely to bite.

FRUSTRATION SET ERIN'S nerves on edge. She hadn't expected much from the Citizen's Police Academy, since she was convinced that Terlecki had started it to promote the glowing image he constantly tried to sell of the police department. He had some reporters convinced *he* was great and wonderful; the local television networks fawned over him.

Erin had intended to make the most of joining the program, but even when the district captains and the chief had introduced the officers of the Lakewood Police

Department, the public information officer had been the one who'd answered or evaded her questions.

"Chief," she called out as she followed the giant of a man down the corridor leading away from the conference room. After the chief had given his speech, the watch commander had called for a break.

Chief Archer stopped midstride and glanced at Erin over his broad shoulder. "Ms. Powell, can I help you?"

"Yes," she said, some of her frustration easing now that she had him alone. "You can answer some of my questions."

Archer grinned the infamous trust-inspiring grin that had probably helped him earn the top spot in the department at a relatively young age. "You have more? It seems Sergeant Terlecki answered everything you asked during class."

"Not the ones about him," she pointed out.

The chief tilted his head, studying her. "What would you like to know about the sergeant?"

"How did he get his cushy job as your public information officer?"

The chief's grin faded. "He earned it, Ms. Powell."

"How? What did he have to do to become your *golden boy?*" she persisted. The nickname she'd given Terlecki fit him more aptly than Bullet. "How many innocent people did he have to arrest?" *Besides her brother.*

The chief's jaw grew taut. "You really know nothing about the sergeant, Ms. Powell."

She knew more than they thought she did. Even if Terlecki remembered Mitchell, he wouldn't connect her to her half brother because of their different last names. Despite the year she'd spent scrutinizing the sergeant's reports, she hadn't found the proof she needed to free Mitchell. "He didn't hold the Lakewood Police Department arrest record before his promotion?"

"Ms. Powell, the sergeant is—"

"The one who's supposed to be answering your questions," Terlecki interjected as he joined them in the hallway. "Thank you, sir. I know you're in a hurry, so I'll handle Ms. Powell."

The chief sighed. "Kent, you should just tell her—"

Terlecki interrupted again with a shake of his head, then waved off his boss as if Kent was the superior officer.

"Tell me what?" Erin asked as he wrapped his fingers around her wrist and drew her down the hall.

"Nothing you need to know," he said dismissively.

Since she'd started at the *Chronicle,* he had been trying to dismiss her. She tugged on her wrist, but his grasp tightened. "So this is how you're going to 'handle' me?"

After leading her into an empty room, Kent closed the door, then released her. "I'd hardly risk an accusation of police brutality, Ms. Powell. I simply thought you'd like some privacy for your interview."

Shut inside a small room with no furniture, only cardboard boxes sitting about, Erin realized how completely alone they were. Terlecki stood between her and the door, blocking her escape. Unnerved, she licked her lips and repeated his last word. "Interview?"

"You were asking the chief about me," he said, his deep voice vibrating with a hint of innuendo, as if her interest in him was personal.

Which it was, but not in the way his ego must have led him to believe.

"I—I..." she stammered, heat rushing to her face with shame and annoyance that she had let him rattle her.

"You don't want to ask *me* about me?" he asked, his gray eyes glinting with amusement.

"You don't answer my questions, Sergeant," she reminded him.

"Because they're not pertinent."

"That's not for you to decide," she pointed out.

"That you're impertinent?"

She bit her lip to hold in a reaction to his insult. She couldn't let him get to her anymore; he was already much too arrogant. "It's not for you to decide what the public needs to know."

"The public?" He arched a blond brow. "I don't think the public cares how I came by my *cushy* job." He stepped closer. "Why do *you* care, Ms. Powell?"

Despite the adrenaline causing her legs to tremble, Erin refused to back away. "I'm a reporter, Sergeant."

"You don't need to remind me of that." Kent wasn't likely to forget, when all she'd ever done was fire questions at him. But sometimes, noticing how her eyes sparkled and her skin flushed when she argued with him, he forgot that she was a reporter who seemed to hate his guts, and he saw her as an exciting woman.

"Being a reporter, I have certain instincts," she continued, as if he hadn't spoken, "which are screaming at me that there's a story behind your made-up position in the department."

"Made-up?"

"Public information officer?" she scoffed. "That hardly sounds like a real job."

He stepped closer, until his badge brushed her

shoulder. She was tall, even without the low heels she wore, and slender, in black pants and a lightweight red sweater. Pitching his voice low, he asked, "What do you know about positions, Ms. Powell?"

Her eyes widening, Erin stumbled back. "Sergeant!"

"Positions within the department," he explained, as if he hadn't baited her, as if he didn't enjoy rattling her cage. Hell, that was the most exciting part of his *cushy* job. Although she was a pain in the ass, she wasn't boring. "What did you think I meant?"

"I'm never sure," she admitted. "You talk out of both sides of your mouth."

He grinned at her insult. "Then I guess I'm good at my *made-up* position."

"So you admit it was?"

Kent swallowed a groan. He probably shouldn't have talked to her at all, let alone dragged her into an empty room. "And you wonder why I don't answer your questions…."

"Since you're not going to, let me out of here." Erin pushed past him to open the door and step into the hall. Beyond the conference room, in the atrium, the elevator dinged. She watched the doors close on most of the CPA participants, on their way to the ground floor.

"Look what you made me do," she declared. "I missed the last part of the class."

"Just tonight's," he reminded her. "You have fourteen more to go."

"You're not going to get me kicked out of the program?"

After what he'd heard her asking the chief, he admitted, "I'd love to."

"I'm sure you would. But you said you're not in charge of the academy, remember?" she taunted.

No one had ever antagonized him as she did, not even some of the belligerent drunks he'd pulled over during his years as a patrol officer. All he had to do to get her tossed from the program was tell Paddy he'd changed his mind. And Kent was damn tempted to do just that.

"So what are you in charge of, as *public information officer?*" she asked. "Damage control?"

"You."

"You're only here to muzzle me? Did you purposely keep me from the second half of the program? Is there something you didn't want me to hear?" She fired the questions in her usual manner, without giving him time to answer one before she moved to the next.

He couldn't get her thrown out of the program. She would never let up on the department—or him—if he did. But he hadn't approved her application because he feared what she would print. He wanted to change her opinion of the department. The chief and his fellow officers worked hard for the community; they didn't deserve the bad press she'd been giving them.

"You can find out what you've missed. I'll take you where they've all probably gone," he offered.

"Home," she scoffed.

"No. There's another place." Where officers went before or after their shifts, to eat, relax and just hang out with people who understood the complexities of doing their job. They wouldn't appreciate his bringing her there. "Just don't make me regret this…."

"YOU BROUGHT ME TO A BAR? This lighthouse is a tavern?" she asked as she passed through the door he held open for her. While all conversation didn't cease as it had at the police department earlier, some people stopped talking and turned toward her and the sergeant. But the jukebox continued to play, over the sounds of several conversations and raucous laughter.

"It's the Lighthouse Bar and Grille," he replied, probably thinking she hadn't seen the sign when they'd pulled into the parking lot in their respective cars.

The mingled aromas of burgers, steaks and salty fries filled the air. Peanut shells crunched beneath her feet as she followed Kent across the room toward a long table near the game area. Several members of the Citizen's Police Academy sat together. She glanced around and noticed that except for those civilian patrons, the rest of the faces were familiar from law enforcement.

"How have I never known about this place?" she wondered aloud. She'd been living here a year. How had she not known that the Lakewood PD hung out at a lighthouse on the Lake Michigan shore? She'd asked around if there was any place the officers frequented, but no one had told her about this place. Out of loyalty to Terlecki?

"You don't exactly inspire confidences," Kent pointed out.

"So why did you bring me here?" she asked.

His lips lifted in a slight grin. "Where did you think I was leading you? Off the pier?"

"Of course. Right into the lake." She had considered

that might be what he'd had in mind. "Don't tell me you weren't tempted."

"Trying to put words in my mouth again, Ms. Powell?"

"There isn't room for me to put words," she insisted. "Not with your foot there most of the time."

He shook his head and laughed. "Nice try, but you're not going to get to me."

"We both know I *get* to you," she said, "but then I don't expect you to admit that." She had to find some other way to extract the truth from him, because she had a horrible feeling he'd covered his tracks too well for her to get the evidence she needed. And if she didn't find proof, she couldn't help the man who mattered most to her.

"Erin," Kent began, but he wasn't the only one calling her name.

She ignored him, leaving his side to join the other members of the CPA. An older couple who had admitted joining the program for thrills waved at her. "Look," the woman, Bernie, said. "We're just like the police officers."

Most of Erin's classmates sat around the table, except for two teachers, the youth minister and the saleswoman who'd, thankfully, taken the chair between Erin and the college girl before class started. The participants all beamed as if they felt a sense of belonging—a sense that Erin envied, doubting she would ever feel it herself. Most of Lakewood, out of loyalty to the police department or Kent personally, disapproved of her articles.

The college girl who had earlier interrupted her conversation with Terlecki grabbed Erin's arm and pulled her down onto a chair beside her. "What's going on with you two?" she asked, her voice giddy with curiosity. She turned away from Erin, tracking Terlecki's long strides toward the bar.

"Uh..." Erin searched her memory for the girl's name from the introduction part of the class. "Amy. Nothing's going on, really."

The woman sitting on the other side of Erin snorted in derision.

Amy giggled. "See, everyone knows that you two have something going on."

"No, we don't," Erin insisted.

"But you both disappeared during the class, then you just walked in together," the blonde stated, unwilling to let it drop.

"Come on," the other woman said, pulling Erin to her feet. Despite her thin build, her grip was strong. And despite her youthful appearance, fine lines on her fair skin betrayed her age as probably almost twice the college girl's. "Let's play darts."

Erin followed, willing to use any excuse to escape the nosy girl, even though she hadn't thrown darts since she had with her older brother. And now she couldn't play with him...thanks to Kent Terlecki, who had sent Mitchell to prison for a crime he hadn't committed. Mitchell would have never dealt drugs.

"I'm surprised you walked in at all," the older woman mused, "let alone with Sergeant Terlecki." She pulled darts from the board and stepped back. Like Amy, she had long blond hair, but a couple of silver strands shone among the platinum. "I thought he'd finally gotten rid of you."

Erin turned toward her, surprised by her barely veiled animosity. She expected it from police officers, but not civilians, although some of them weren't shy about telling her she was wrong. "I'm sorry. I don't remember your name."

"Marla. Marla Halliday." She waited, as if Erin was supposed to recognize her name. Then she added, "My son is a police officer—Sergeant Bartholomew 'Billy' Halliday with the vice unit."

The name still meant nothing to Erin—it hadn't come up in any of her research—but the woman's attitude made complete sense now. "Oh."

"Yeah. *Oh.* When you attack the department, you're attacking every one of those hardworking officers—not just Sergeant Terlecki," Marla admonished, with a mother's fierce protectiveness.

"I'm sure your son is a fine officer, but—"

"That's your problem, honey. You're *sure* regardless of the facts. You're *sure* even when you're wrong." Marla's porcelain skin reddened. "Not that my son isn't a fine officer, because he is. But he's not Sergeant Terlecki."

"Then he *is* a fine officer." He wouldn't frame a man for a crime he hadn't committed just to pad his arrest record and further his career, as Kent Terlecki had.

"But Billy's not a hero," his mother said.

"You're saying Sergeant Terlecki—*Kent* Terlecki is a hero?"

Marla nodded. "Why do you think they call him Bullet?"

"I have no idea." The mystery of his nickname had been bugging her since she had moved to the west Michigan town of Lakewood. "Why don't you tell me?"

"Hey, Ms. Halliday," Kent said as he joined them.

"Do you have some kind of radar for whenever I ask a question?" Erin asked, her stomach knotted with frustration over how close she'd come to learning one of his secrets before he'd thwarted her again.

"You have to be careful of this one," Kent said to Marla Halliday. "She tries to interview everyone."

"No interview here," Marla said. "We were just going to play darts." Her blue eyes twinkled. Kent grimaced, but she ignored him. "Here, Erin, why don't you go first?"

Erin closed her fingers around the proffered bunch of brightly colored darts. She chose one to throw, then turned to the board to find someone had pinned a blown-up picture of *her* there.

Not someone. *Him.*

Kent Terlecki was *no* hero.

Chapter Two

A chuckle at the shocked expression on her face rumbled in Kent's chest, but he suppressed it. Instead he moved up behind her, then closed his hand around her fingers holding the dart.

"See?" he said as he lifted her hand and guided the throw. "A bull's-eye is right between the eyes."

"*My* eyes," she muttered. As the dart pierced the paper across the bridge of her nose, she winced.

"Your chin and ears are five points, your mouth and cheeks ten and your—"

"I get the idea," she interrupted, tugging her hand free and stepping away.

He hadn't realized he was still holding her. Or that Billy's mom had left them, to return to the others. Maybe it was good he wasn't out in the field anymore. His instincts were not as sharp as they'd once been.

"And I *get* to you," she said, "whether you're willing to admit it or not."

"Why?" He asked the question that had been nagging at him for a year.

"*Why* do I get to you?" she asked, her lips tilting

up in a smug smile. "Or *why* aren't you willing to tell the truth?"

"*Why* do you want to get to me?" he wondered. "I'm always the victim of your poison pen."

"A little paranoid, Sergeant?" she teased, her dark eyes gleaming with amusement. And triumph.

He shook his head. "No. I used to think it wasn't personal. That I was your target just because I represented the department."

"Now you're a martyr," she quipped.

Remembering all those people who had tried to make him one, he suppressed a shudder. "God, no."

"Oh, I forgot. You're a *hero*," she said. "That's what Mrs. Halliday called you."

The act that others called heroic had been sheer instinct—an instinct every cop had. He didn't doubt that any one of his fellow officers would have done the same thing he had. "I'm no hero."

"You don't have to tell *me* that."

He clenched his jaw so hard that his back teeth ground together. The woman was damn infuriating. "So it is personal."

"You're paranoid," she said, but her gaze slid away from his.

"I heard what you said to the chief," he admitted. "That you think I got my job by arresting innocent people. Why would you ask that?"

Sure, a lot of people claimed innocence, but no one he'd arrested had ever gotten away with their crimes. There'd always been too much evidence.

She shrugged. "How else would you have racked up the arrest record you have?"

"Because a lot of people commit crimes, Ms. Powell." He stated what he considered obvious. "And I'm good at catching them."

"Not anymore," she taunted. "You sit behind a desk now. Your badge is all for show."

Damn, she had struck that nerve he'd sworn she couldn't. But she had actually spoken a grain of truth for once. Sometimes he did feel as if his badge were only a prop.

Her eyes sparkled as if she'd picked up on her direct hit to his pride. "Isn't that what you wanted?" she asked. "To move up in the department, to get ahead?"

Getting *desked* was the last thing he'd wanted, but she was the last person to whom he would make that confession. "I know what you think of me, however unfounded," Kent said. "Do you know what I think of you?"

"I can guess," she replied, gesturing toward the dartboard.

He shook his head. "That wasn't my idea. Someone else blew up the photo that runs with your byline, and pinned it there." *For* him. He couldn't claim that he hadn't appreciated the gesture, though.

"I don't care what you think of me, Sergeant," she insisted.

"I'm going to tell you anyway," he assured her.

"On the record or off?"

"Everything seems to go on the record with you." Which he would come to regret, he knew.

"The public has a right to know…."

"Do they know about you?" he wondered. "That you're ambitious to the point of ruthless? That you'll use anything and anyone to further your career?"

She shook her head. "The person you just described sounds more like you. You don't know me at all, Sergeant."

"Then I guess we're even."

He finally admitted to himself the rest of his reason for allowing her into the program. He hadn't wanted to change her opinion of just the department—he'd wanted to change her opinion of him, too. After a year of trying to deal with her, he should have known better. She was a lost cause.

ERIN TIPTOED INTO her dark apartment as if she were a kid sneaking in past curfew. And just like when she was a kid, she got caught. A lamp snapped on and flooded the living room with light.

Was this *actually* her apartment? Someone had tidied up. Books had been put back on the built-in cherrywood shelves. Nothing but polish covered the hardwood floor. Even the cushions were on the couch. If not for having just unlocked the door, she would have suspected she'd stumbled into the wrong place.

"You're late," Kathryn Powell pointed out from where she sat primly, with her ankles crossed, on the sofa. Had her mother been sleeping like that or just sitting in the dark, waiting for her?

Erin blinked against the glare of the halogen bulb of the floor lamp. "I'm sorry."

She should have called, but she hadn't planned to go anywhere after class. Once she'd arrived at the Lighthouse, she hadn't dared to call, what with the rowdy background noise. Her mother would have gotten the wrong idea. She tended to think the worst of her children.

Kathryn sniffed as if doubting Erin's sincerity, and

patted her short brown hair, not a single strand of which was displaced. "Your father is upset that I'm not home yet. He doesn't want me making that long drive alone at this hour."

Her parents lived about seventy miles southeast of Lakewood, in the austere Tudor home where Erin and her older brother, Mitchell, had grown up, in East Grand Rapids. Her brother had moved to Lakewood for college, and then, after dropping out, had stayed on because he'd liked being close to the water.

"You can stay over," Erin offered, although her shoulders tensed at the thought of more *quality time* with Mom. Despite her mother's best efforts, she would never be able to tidy up Erin's life.

Kathryn shook her head. "I didn't bring any of my things with me. I didn't think your class was supposed to go so late."

"It wasn't." It hadn't. "Or I wouldn't have signed up. You can stay, Mom. You can borrow something of mine."

"No, I need to get home to your father."

Mitchell had resented their mother's devotion to Erin's dad, his stepfather. That devotion used to inspire Erin to want that kind of love for herself someday, but she'd given up on her dream of love for her dream of *justice.* She had to clear Mitchell's name and get his conviction overturned.

Erin passed through the neat living room to the hall, traveling a few steps to lean against the doorjamb of a bedroom. A night-light with a clown's face illuminated a jumble of blocks and cars littering the racetrack rug. She ignored the clutter and focused on the bed and the small body curled into a ball under the covers.

"How was he?" she asked her mother, who had followed her—despite her desire to get home to her husband.

Kathryn sighed. "Hyperactive. And much too dependent on you."

Guilt surpassed the defensiveness her mother usually inspired in her, and Erin admitted, "Maybe I shouldn't have signed up for the course."

Kathryn stepped closer and sniffed her hair. "You smell like you've been in a bar instead of a classroom."

Erin shook her head. "Restaurant. It was easier to do interviews there than at the police department." Or it would have been if she'd actually managed to speak to anyone without Sergeant Terlecki's interference.

"You're wasting your time," her mother claimed. "If what you're really looking for is some evidence to clear your brother, you're not going to find anything."

"Mom, I have to *help* him." She would never be able to turn her back on her half brother the way her parents had. "Not just for Mitchell but for Jason, too. He can't keep losing people he loves."

That was why her nephew had become so attached to Erin—he was afraid she would leave him, as his father had four years ago and then his mother just last year. Mitchell's girlfriend had found someone else, someone who didn't want to raise another man's child. So except for Erin's parents, who tended to be more disapproving than affectionate, Erin was all the little boy had now.

"If you want to help your brother," Kathryn advised, "then get him to admit the truth."

"He's not the one lying." Kent Terlecki was. He had to be, or else her brother was one of those many people of whom Kent had spoken who committed crimes. And her older brother, *her* hero growing up, could *not* be a criminal.

A CURSE BROKE THE SILENCE in the living room, then books and CDs toppled to the hardwood floor as someone banged into a table in the dark. Kent snapped on a lamp, the light revealing the intruder: a tall, wiry guy with dark hair and a beard, dressed in dark clothes.

"What the hell—" Billy griped as he rubbed his knee. "Why are you sitting up in the dark?"

"Couldn't sleep."

"Your back bothering you?"

Kent shook his head. "Nope," he said, ignoring the twinge along his spine. He had grown used to it over the past few years. "That's not the pain keeping me awake."

"The reporter?" Billy asked, snorting with disgust.

He nodded.

"I heard you brought her to the Lighthouse." Billy dropped onto the old plaid couch across from the leather chair where Kent sat.

"You talked to your mom?" He grinned as he thought of Marla Halliday and how she'd led Erin to the dartboard. "Did you know she was joining the class?"

Billy shook his head. "I wish Paddy would've given me the heads-up he gave you about Powell."

"You're lucky you have a mom who wants to be involved in what you're doing," Kent told him. He'd been estranged from his folks since he'd chosen to go to the police academy instead of continuing the Terlecki tradition of working the family farm in northern Michigan.

"Mom *can't* be involved in my life now," Billy said, sinking deeper into the couch. Exhaustion blackened the skin beneath his eyes, making him look older than his twenty-six years. "You know how vice is…."

Deep cover. Streets. Bars. Abandoned houses and back alleys. Late nights and dangerous people. Kent had *loved* his years in vice. That was where he had made the majority of his arrests. Erin was delusional to think he'd had to frame innocent people; he hadn't met many innocent people during that time. Or now. Somehow he suspected she was every bit as dangerous as the criminals he'd dealt with during his stint in vice.

She sure had it in for him for some reason, finding fault with everything he said or did.

"How come you came home?" Kent asked.

Not that Billy spent every night in the drug house the department had set up in the seedy area of Lakewood. The cover wasn't so deep that the officers weren't entitled to some downtime. Some officers even worked a regular twelve-hour shift. Billy wasn't one of them.

The other man yawned and flopped his head against the back of the sofa. "I wanted to get some sleep without having to keep one eye open to watch my back."

"I remember feeling like that," Kent sympathized.

"You should still feel like that," his roommate warned him, "with that reporter out to get you. Why the hell did you okay Erin Powell getting into the CPA?"

He sighed. "I wanted to prove to her that the department has nothing to hide."

"She's not as interested in the department as she is you, Bullet," Billy warned him. Some of the weariness left his dark eyes as he leaned forward and studied Kent. "You're not interested in her, are you?"

Kent choked on a laugh. "Talk about having to sleep with one eye open…"

Not that he expected they would do much sleeping if they ever stopped fighting. Erin Powell was one passionate woman. Too bad her passion was hating him.

"We're talking Fatal Attraction, huh?" Billy chuckled.

"Oh, yeah," Kent agreed. *For me.* How the heck could he be attracted to a woman who obviously couldn't stand him? Especially since he really didn't like her much, either. But she was so damn beautiful….

"So why the hell did you bring her to the 'house?" Billy asked again, too good an officer to give up.

But after serving as public information officer for three years, Kent was good at sidestepping questions he didn't want to answer. "She saw the picture you pinned to the dartboard," he said instead.

Billy chuckled again. "That should be a warning to her to lay off. You showed her?"

"Your mom did."

The younger man sighed. "Yeah, now that my mom knows where the 'house is, there'll be no escaping her."

"Your mom is great," Kent countered, staunchly defending Marla Halliday. "And tough." She'd had Billy when she was seventeen, and had raised him all by herself.

"She's not your mom," Billy reminded him.

That hadn't stopped Kent from wishing he'd had someone like her in his life—someone who actually gave a damn about him. "You're lucky."

His friend sighed. "Yeah, I am. Too bad you didn't have better luck."

As well as not being a hero, he wasn't a martyr, either. He refused to blame anyone else or make any excuses for what had happened to him. "We make our own luck."

"By letting Powell into the program, you made yourself some bad luck, my friend," Billy warned. "You're going to have no escape from her now."

It didn't much matter where Erin went. He already had no escape from her. She was in his head…and under his skin.

"Why'd you bring her there?" Billy persisted.

Kent shrugged, keeping the grimace from his face as muscles tightened in his back. "I don't know."

"You want to get her to change her mind about you," the younger officer guessed correctly.

"About the department," Kent insisted, unwilling to admit everything.

After all the things she'd written about him, Erin Powell should be the last woman to whom Kent was attracted. But his instincts told him there was something more to her, something she didn't want him to know. And he'd never been able to resist a mystery. Of course, his instincts had gotten too rusty to trust, so he could be wrong. He might have just imagined the hint of vulnerability in her brown eyes.

His roommate remarked, "Seems like her biggest problem is with you."

"Seems like," he agreed.

Billy leaned back on the sofa again and closed his

eyes, almost idly asking, “So are you going to finally find out why she has a problem with you?”

“How?” She was too stubborn to tell him.

“You may have been desked, but you’re still one of the best cops Lakewood’s ever had. You know how,” his roommate insisted.

“Beat a confession out of her?” Kent asked with a laugh. “That’s the kind of cop she seems to think I was.”

“She doesn’t know a damn thing about you.”

“No.” And she seemed to think he didn’t know a thing about her. Maybe it was time—past time, actually—that he did. He wanted to know everything there was to know about Erin Powell.

Chapter Three

Erin's hand trembled as she closed it around the door handle of the editor-in-chief's office. When she had come into the *Chronicle*—late *again*—she had found a note on her desk ordering her to see Mr. Stein immediately. He stood in front of the windows looking out over the rain-slicked city of Lakewood, his back to her. Quaint brick buildings lined the cobblestone streets, and in the distance whitecaps rose on Lake Michigan, slapping against the shoreline.

She cleared the nervousness from her voice. "Sir? You wanted to see me?"

"You finally made it in?" he asked, without turning toward her.

"I was working from home, sir," she said, hoping to pacify him with the partial truth. "I do some of my best work from home."

The heavyset man finally left the windows and dropped into the leather chair behind his desk. On his blotter was a printout of the article she had turned in the day before: Public Information Officer Admits Cushy Job a Made-Up Position. "The reason I wanted to talk to you is because I've been getting complaints about you."

So she wasn't being called on the carpet over her tardiness this time. She winced as if she could feel the dart between her eyes. "Let me guess—Sergeant Terlecki?"

"No, surprisingly," Herb Stein said as he leaned back, his chair creaking in protest due to his substantial weight. "I think he's the only one who hasn't complained."

Erin's face heated. "Then…who?"

"Just about everyone else down at the department, and quite a lot of the general public."

She wasn't surprised. She hadn't been welcomed very warmly by anyone at the class or the bar afterward a few days before. But still it stung, having people dislike her. Yet she hadn't joined the CPA to make friends; she was after the truth.

"I had some serious doubts about hiring you," Herb admitted. "You didn't have much experience, going from college directly into the Peace Corps."

"I was a journalist with the college paper," she reminded him. "And I wrote several freelance articles while I was in the Corps." She'd been in South America, teaching in a remote village school and helping out at the local clinic and wherever else she had been needed. She hadn't known then how much she'd been needed back home.

"That bleeding heart stuff." He dismissed the work of which she was the proudest. "I didn't think you had it in you to be a *real* journalist. That's why I've kept you on probation."

Dread filled her, but she had to know. "Are you firing me now?"

Her boss laughed. "Hell, no. At least people are reading your byline. That's more than I can say about some of the other staff. I hired you because I thought that even for a bleeding heart, you had potential. That you had some drive."

Jason was her drive. Jason and Mitchell. She had to help them. "I do."

"You've proved me right."

Erin uttered a sigh of relief. "You had me worried that I was losing my job."

"No, in fact, I like this new angle—you attending the Citizen's Police Academy."

"Uh, that's great." She actually wasn't that certain she'd made the right choice in joining. Terlecki wouldn't let anyone but him answer her queries, and he never answered the most important question. Then again, she couldn't ask him outright if he'd framed her brother to pad his arrest record. He was too smart to make any incriminating admissions.

She was also worried about Jason. While the class met only one night a week, he hated being separated from her. Dropping the six-year-old at school every morning had become an ordeal. He claimed to be sick, and since he did have asthma and allergies, she was never certain if he was telling the truth. Her stomach tightened now with guilt over leaving him with his first-grade teacher. While the older woman had assured her that he was always fine the moment Erin left, she was concerned.

"Did you hear me?" Herb asked, his voice sharp with impatience.

"I'm sorry, sir," Erin said, face heating. "What were you saying?"

Her lack of attention apparently forgiven, he grinned. "I'm going to give you your own column to report on what happens while you're in the academy."

Her own column? If she truly were the ambitious reporter Kent thought her, she would be thrilled. Instead, nervous tension coursed through her. Could she handle a column, in addition to her regular coverage of the police beat and taking care of her nephew?

"Thank you, sir," she finally murmured, "I hope I don't disappoint you."

"Just keep writing like this," he said, slapping his hand on the copy of her last article. He chuckled with glee. "I love it."

"I HATE IT."

The chief chuckled as he settled onto the chair behind his desk. "I think the feeling's mutual."

"I said I hate *it,*" Kent clarified as he paced the small space between the chief's desk and the paneled office walls. "I hate the *article,* not her."

But it wasn't just an article anymore—she had been given her own column: Powell on Patrol, which was to be like a weekly journal of her adventures in the Citizen's Police Academy.

"I suspect her boss and my *friend* the mayor had something to do with this," the chief admitted. He and the mayor were hardly friends, more like barely civil enemies.

Kent suspected their animosity had something to do with the chief's wife, since the mayor had pretty much dropped any civility since her death a year ago. "Joel Standish does own the *Chronicle* and control Herb Stein."

"Yeah, but I don't think they're twisting her arm to

write this stuff. She really seems to hate you." The chief slapped the paper against his desk. "I'd hate her, too, if I were you." Anger flushed the older man's face.

Kent laughed at his even-mannered boss expressing such a sentiment. Maybe Kent didn't have the loving family his roommate had, but the department was his family, and there was no one more loyal than a fellow officer. "That's you."

"C'mon, you have to hate her," Frank Archer insisted. "Look at how she twisted your words."

Kent took the proffered paper from his boss's outstretched hand. "I read it." He didn't even glance at the column as he recited from memory, "'Public information officer Sergeant Terlecki admits his cushy job at the Lakewood Police Department is a made-up position.'"

"She did twist your words, right?" The chief leaned forward. "Because I remember you saying something pretty similar when I offered you the job."

"We hadn't had a public information officer before," Kent reminded him. The chief—and his predecessor—had always handled the press themselves. If he'd been too busy, his secretary had claimed he wasn't available for comment.

"But other departments that aren't even as big as ours have public information officers to deal with the media, and we should, too," Frank insisted. "We needed one. We needed *you*."

Kent stopped his pacing and held the man's pale blue gaze. "You didn't create the job because..."

"Because you took a bullet for me?" The chief shook his head. "Son, I'd take it back if I could."

"The job?" He deliberately misunderstood, his lips twitching into a smile.

"The *bullet*."

"Nobody can take the bullet out." Not without a seventy-five percent chance of leaving him paralyzed. Those weren't odds Kent was willing to take a risk on; as Billy had said, he wasn't lucky.

"Have you checked with a surgeon recently?" Chief Archer asked. "There are new medical advances all the time. You could go to the University of Michigan or the Mayo—"

"I'm fine, really," he assured his boss, whom he also thought of as a friend. Despite Kent's insistence, he knew that Frank Archer would always feel guilty that Kent had gotten hurt while protecting him.

"You're bored out of your mind in this job," the chief stated.

Apparently Kent hadn't done very well hiding his dissatisfaction. He tapped a finger against the newspaper he held. "Erin Powell keeps things interesting."

The chief's pale eyes narrowed. "Not interesting enough, I suspect. I know you, Kent. I know you'd rather be back in the field."

"So put me back in the field," Kent snapped, tired of hiding his feelings to spare others' guilt.

Betraying his inner torment, the chief closed his eyes and shook his head. "God, I wish I could, Kent, but I can't, not without medical clearance."

"I'm sorry," Kent said, as his own guilt coursed through him. He hadn't wanted to make the chief feel worse than he already did. "I know you can't." With the bullet so close to his spine, he was too much of a liability.

Even without surgery, there was a risk of paralysis from scar tissue pressing on nerves or the bullet moving and irrevocably damaging his spinal cord. It wouldn't be fair to his fellow officers—the ones he might need to back up—or to the civilians he might need to protect if he was on the job. Erin had been exactly right the other night when she'd claimed that his badge was just for show.

The chief sighed, then forced a smile. "At least Erin Powell keeps you from being bored senseless in your *cushy* job."

"That she does." Kent gripped the paper tighter and glanced down at the picture of her next to the byline of her new column. While he didn't betray it to his boss, anger gripped him. He wanted to wring her pretty little neck. She had deliberately twisted every damn word he'd spoken to her the other night.

"You should tell her," the chief advised.

"How I came by my nickname?" Kent shook his head. "No, we agreed to keep that from the public."

"Back then. Three years ago. Keeping it secret was your first decision as public information officer." The chief's eyes filled with pride. "You were on your way to surgery at the time."

The surgery hadn't removed the bullet, though the doctors still claimed they had saved his life. But Kent couldn't do his job anymore, so he had no life. At least not the life he used to have—the one he wanted.

"It was a good decision," Kent insisted. Keeping the attempt on the chief's life quiet *had* been a good decision, but maybe he should have had the bullet taken out, and risked paralysis.

"You really *don't* want the public to make you a hero," the chief mused, shaking his head.

"Not when someone else has to be the villain."

"But the woman *shot* you!" The older man's voice shook with emotion.

"She was trying to shoot *you,*" Kent reminded him. "I think we both agree that Mrs. Ludlowe paid for what she did. It wouldn't be fair to open up all that pain again." And reporters like Erin Powell would be only too happy to do that. He tossed the paper onto the chief's cluttered desk.

Frank leaned back in his chair and sighed, then grabbed the paper and crumpled it up. "*This* is not fair to you. You're taking another bullet that isn't meant for you."

Kent grinned. "Oh, I have a feeling this bullet is meant *only* for me."

"Why?"

He shrugged. "I don't know, but I'm going to find out. It's past time I learned." He was going to take Billy's advice, polish up his rusty investigative skills and finally figure out what Erin Powell's problem was with him.

"Be careful, Kent," the chief advised. "You haven't been out in the field for a while."

"Doesn't matter." He waved dismissively and headed for the door. "I've been dodging Erin Powell's bullets for a year now."

"You haven't dodged them all, Bullet," the chief reminded him. "Be careful."

ERIN JOLTED, and her computer slid from her lap onto the floor in front of the couch. "Da—" She swallowed the curse as the door rattled again under a hammering fist. She scrambled toward it, pulling it open with a "Shh…!"

Her heart pounded harder at the sight of the man leaning against the jamb. Instead of his black uniform, he wore faded jeans and a black leather jacket over a T-shirt that had molded to the impressive muscles of his chest. His hair was a darker blond, damp from a shower.

She swallowed a traitorous sigh. "Oh, it's you…."

"You shouldn't open your door before you know who's on the other side," Sergeant Terlecki chastised her.

"You're lucky I didn't know who was pounding down my door," she pointed out. "What do you want, Sergeant?" She noted the wrinkled newspaper he clutched. "Are you here to congratulate me on my new column?"

He crumpled the paper in his fist. "What I want is a retraction."

She shook her head, then tucked a stray strand of hair behind her ear. "I can't."

"What do you have against me, Erin? What have I ever done to you? I'm too old to have gone to school with you and ignored you."

Just. He was only five years older than she was, but she refrained from mentioning that.

He leaned closer until his handsome face was mere inches from hers. "And if I'd gone to school with you, I know I would *never* have ignored you."

She couldn't fight the smile curving her lips. So his new method for handling her was to turn on his infamous charm, which served him so well with the network reporters. "You're *flirting* with me now?"

"Don't act so surprised," he admonished with a grin of his own. "I've flirted with you before."

"You have?" She widened her eyes in disbelief. "When was that? When you dragged me into an empty room? When you pinned my picture to a dartboard?"

"You didn't know I was flirting?" He clicked his tongue against his teeth. "I must have gotten rusty."

"No, I can't believe..." She lifted her hand to push back her hair again, but this time her fingers trembled, so she propped her hand on her hip. She couldn't let him get to her. "Why—why would you flirt with me? You must hate me."

That steely gaze of his focused on her. "You want me to hate you."

No, *she* wanted to hate *him.* How could she not, after what he'd done?

"I should," he said. "It's pretty clear you have it in for me." He tossed the torn newspaper atop the cluttered table just inside her foyer. "I want to know why."

"I thought you knew."

He grinned. "That you're ambitious, that you'll do anything to get ahead? Yeah, I know that. But I think there's more to you, Erin Powell—more to *us*."

She started to swing the door shut on his handsome face. "There is no us."

He pressed his palm against the panel, holding it open. "Oh, there's something here."

"Hatred, remember?" She levered her weight against the door, but it still didn't move, his hand holding it effortlessly.

He shook his head. "I don't hate you."

"Give me time."

His brow furrowed with confusion. "So you are out to destroy me?"

"I think it's only fair." Since he had destroyed her brother's life and a little boy's whole world.

"Why, Erin?" Kent asked, as if it bothered him, as if he cared what she thought, what she felt. "What did I ever do to you?"

Maybe she should tell him, so he would understand that flirting with her was a waste of his time and hers. She only wanted one thing from him—the truth. "You—"

A cry caught Erin's attention. The fear in it had her whirling away and racing down the hall, calling out, "It's okay. I'm here…."

Stunned, Kent stepped inside the open door. It hadn't occurred to him that she might not live alone. She didn't wear a wedding band or even an engagement ring. He had checked the first time he'd met the beauty at a press conference—before she'd started with her impertinent questions.

Curious, and concerned about the cry, he followed her. He stumbled over toys in the hall outside the doorway where she'd disappeared. Inside the room she knelt beside a twin bed, her arms wrapped tight around a small, trembling body.

Kent slipped quietly into the bedroom. She was totally unaware of his presence as she focused on the boy, who must have been about five or six. Since speaking at school assemblies was part of his duties as public information officer, Kent spent a lot of time around kids now. Before he'd been injured, the thought of doing so would have scared him more than getting shot, but talking to schoolkids had actually become one of the high points of his new job. The children sometimes asked tougher questions than reporters, though. Well, all reporters besides Erin Powell.

He never would have imagined that aggressive journalist was the same woman who cuddled the crying child, soothing him with a calming voice and a tender touch. A part of Kent had suspected there was more to Erin Powell, something softer and more vulnerable—something that had attracted his interest in spite of her animosity toward him.

She pressed her lips to the boy's forehead. "Shh…"

Now Kent understood her shushing him at the door. She hadn't wanted to disturb the boy. Was he her son?

"Go back to sleep, Jason," she urged the whimpering child. "Everything's okay."

The boy sniffled. "I heard somebody yelling."

"It was nothing, honey," Erin said, her voice filled with a gentleness Kent would not have considered her capable of. "Nothing for you to worry about."

"But I heard a *guy,*" Jason said, as if having a man in Erin's apartment was unusual. "He was *yelling* at you."

"I'm sorry about that." Kent spoke up from the shadows of the room.

Both the child and Erin tensed and turned toward him. "You shouldn't have followed me," she told him. "You shouldn't have just walked in."

"I'm sorry," Kent repeated to the boy, ignoring her irritation that he had let himself inside her apartment. He would not argue with her in front of the child.

She opened her mouth, then closed it, as if coming to the same realization.

"I wasn't yelling. Really," Kent assured the child. "I

was just talking loud. I didn't know you were sleeping." He hadn't known about the kid at all.

"Who are you?" the little boy asked, staring up at Kent with wide eyes that were the same shade of chocolate-brown as Erin's.

"I'm Serge—"

"He's a friend," Erin interrupted. "Now you have to go back to sleep, honey. You have school in the morning." She pulled the covers up to the boy's chin and kissed his forehead. With his dark hair and those eyes and delicate features, he looked very much like Erin.

A pressure shifted in Kent's chest, releasing some of his resentment toward her. He'd been right—there was much more to Erin Powell than she was willing to reveal.

She rose from her knees and reached out, grasping Kent's arm to pull him from the room. He could have resisted her effort to give him the bum's rush, but he followed, admiring the swing of her narrow hips beneath her cotton pajama bottoms. Instead of a matching top, she wore an old gray sweatshirt.

She didn't speak until they'd left the hall and returned to the living room. "You need to leave," she told him. Although she kept it low, her voice vibrated with anger. "You shouldn't have come here. You have no right to barge into my home."

"You just called me a friend," he reminded her with a grin.

Her eyes narrowed with irritation. "I lied."

"To your son?" Kent had to know—was the boy hers? With the similarity between them, he had to be.

"You have no right to interfere in my life," she protested as she headed straight to the door and opened it. "Where I live, who I live with is none of your business."

"You made it mine with every venomous word you wrote about me." He closed his hand over hers and pressed the door closed. "You're my business now, Erin, so I'm going to find out everything there is to know about you."

She turned toward him, her eyes wide. "You can't—"

"I *can,*" he assured her. "Despite what you think, I'm still a *real* cop."

"Have you forgotten a little thing called freedom of the press?" she asked. "I won't stop writing about you. You can't intimidate me."

"No, I can't," he agreed. "Unless you have something to hide, something you don't want me to find out."

Chapter Four

"I have nothing to hide," she lied, her breath catching. She didn't want him to know anything about her, most especially not about her brother. If Kent knew what she was after, he would cover his tracks even better than he already had. She'd gone over and over all his arrest records and had found nothing to help Mitchell. Yet.

She tugged her hand free of Kent's and stepped back, trying to put some distance between them.

But he moved closer, his shoulders casting a wide shadow in the foyer. "Nothing?" he asked. "The fact that you have a son is nothing?"

She glanced back at the hall leading to Jason's bedroom. "I never said he's my son."

"He's not?"

She lifted her shoulders in a noncommittal shrug. "I could just be babysitting." Which she was, until she found proof that Terlecki had framed Mitchell.

"He looks so much like you that he must be a relative," Kent said, with such certainty that she lifted a brow.

"My nephew," she admitted, although she had grown to think of him as more than that over the past year.

"And you're not just babysitting him."

She swallowed, her mouth watering from nerves. "You think you know everything," she scoffed, but she was afraid that he soon would.

"Not everything," he said, shaking his head. His hair had completely dried, the strands a pale gold color again. "I know the boy lives with you. He has his own room, and there are toys all over."

"Maybe I'm just a really loving aunt."

"I don't doubt that," he admitted. "I can tell the two of you are very close. Too close for you to be just baby-sitting. You're obviously his principal caregiver, or even his guardian. How did that come about?"

She decided to tell him what she told anyone else nosy enough to push for an answer. "His parents weren't able to care for him anymore."

"What happened?" Kent pressed. "Did they die?"

"They're not dead." Not yet. Although Mitchell had been in prison for four years already, she worried about him being able to survive there much longer. Certainly he wouldn't last the rest of his ten-year sentence.

"Then why can't they care for him anymore?"

Her heart thumped hard. For a year, with no success, she'd been trying to learn Kent's secrets. After less than an hour in her home he was entirely too close to learning hers. "That's none of your business."

He shook his head. "We've been through this already. You've made yourself my business, Erin—" he stepped nearer, his chest bumping her shoulder "—with every article you've written attacking me. And now this *column* of yours—Powell on Patrol…" He snorted in derision.

"You just can't take the truth," she snapped, refusing to allow him to intimidate her. She planted her feet on the hardwood floor so she wouldn't move back, even though her pulse raced with his nearness.

His gunmetal-gray eyes narrowed. "No, I think you're the one who can't take it."

Did he already know the truth? Was it possible that he had talked to her *mother?*

"Just because someone wants you to believe something doesn't make it true," she insisted, tilting up her chin with defiance and pride.

"I hope everyone who reads your articles and your new column realizes that." He lifted his hand and slid his thumb along her jaw. "I'm not the bad guy you want everyone to think I am."

Not everyone. Just herself. She wanted to believe he was the bad guy, but his touch, so gentle against her skin, distracted her.

"You're flirting with me again," she said, reminding herself that turning on the charm was probably just another of his tactics.

"That's not flirting," Kent said as he lowered his head, his face nearing hers. "*This* is flirting...." His mouth touched hers, lips brushing across lips.

Erin's heart shifted, then beat hard and fast. She reached out, intending to push him away, but her palms pressed against the hard wall of his chest. His heart was racing as frantically as hers.

He closed his arms around her, pulling her tight against him, and deepened the kiss.

Erin's lips clung to his, returning his passion with a surge of her own. She opened her mouth, and the tip of his tongue slid across her bottom lip. Heat flashed through her body, yet she shivered.

"Erin…" he murmured, as if uncertain that she was really in his arms.

What the hell am I doing? Disbelief doused her desire. She shoved her hands forcefully against his chest, pushing him back. "No!"

"Erin—"

Remembering her nephew, she lowered her voice and said, "Please, get out…."

She closed her eyes, shame washing over her. How had she forgotten about Jason? How had she forgotten about Mitchell and what Kent had done to him? Taking him away from his son, from *her?*

Kent's hand, shaking slightly, closed around the doorknob. "Erin—"

"Just leave…."

She didn't open her eyes again until she heard the door close behind him. Tears of guilt blurred her vision, the mahogany door wavering in and out of focus. She lifted a hand to her mouth, intending to wipe away every last trace of his kiss, but her lips still tingled with the sensation of his mouth against hers. She licked her lips and tasted *him.*

How could I have enjoyed his kiss? How could I have kissed him back?

She latched the chain and bolted the door, wishing she could lock him out of her mind as easily as she could her apartment. Yet he wouldn't leave, not until she got justice for her brother.

She walked back to her nephew's room, leaning against the doorjamb to study his face in the faint glow of his night-light. He slept peacefully, blissfully unaware of what his aunt had done, and whom she had allowed into their home.

The man who had taken away his father. The man who had given Jason nightmares, because the child had been there four years ago when Sergeant Terlecki, working vice, had led a special response unit into their home. The team had broken down the door and, with their big guns and loud voices, had stormed the apartment.

Just a toddler, Jason had been too young to have a clear memory of that day when Kent had arrested his father. But ever since then, the little boy had had nightmares and a paralyzing fear of police officers.

Erin hadn't feared Kent Terlecki—until tonight. Until he kissed her. And she didn't actually fear him as much as she feared what he had made her feel. *Desire.*

WHAT HAD HE BEEN THINKING?

He walked into the Lighthouse, grateful for the noise that surged out of the open door like a wave. Hopefully, it would be too damn loud for him to think, to replay in his mind what he'd just done.

He had kissed Erin Powell, the reporter determined to destroy him and the department. Or maybe the department was just collateral damage. He would bet that her real intention was to ruin *him.*

Was that why she'd kissed him back? To trick him, to mess with his head? The kiss had been even more effective at doing that than anything she'd written. Yet he suspected he hadn't been the only one that kiss had rattled.

Nodding at people who waved or shouted in greeting, he made his way through the crowd to the bar. The bartender, an auburn-haired beauty named Brigitte, greeted him with a smile. "Hey, Sarge, your usual?"

His usual was Bloody Mary mix on ice, without the alcohol. Tonight he felt like he needed the *bloody*. The bloodier the better. He shook his head. "Shot of tequila."

Brigitte, whom he thought he'd seen the other night at the CPA, lifted a brow. "Really?"

"Really?" Paddy parroted as he swiveled the stool he was sitting on toward Kent. "You don't usually imbibe."

"Not by choice," he murmured as he settled onto the stool beside the lieutenant. Whoever had been using it when he'd walked in had just vacated it. Probably a rookie. Once they heard about the bullet he'd taken for the chief, they treated him differently—almost reverently—which generally got on his nerves.

Maybe the chief was right; maybe he needed to tell Erin what had happened to him so *she* would treat him differently. But then she had, for just a little while, when she'd kissed him back. Before she'd remembered how much she hated him, and had pushed him away.

"You still taking pain pills?" Paddy asked, his eyes darkening with concern.

Kent shrugged. "Not that often." He lifted the shot glass Brigitte set in front of him. "Not tonight." Even the bite of the fiery liquid couldn't burn Erin's taste from his lips. She'd tasted so sweet. How could such a vicious woman taste that good?

Then he remembered how tender she'd been with her nephew, the poor kid whose parents were no longer able to look after him. His aunt obviously cared for him with the same passion with which she'd been going after

Kent in the press. She was only nasty with him. What the hell did she have against him?

"Does it still hurt a lot?"

Her hating him? It shouldn't hurt at all, but it bothered him. She'd been so great with the boy—so loving and generous. He'd suspected there was more to Erin Powell than the beauty that had initially attracted him. Now he knew she had the capacity for compassion and love.

"The bullet," Paddy prodded, as if realizing Kent's mind was somewhere else, on someone else. "Does it still hurt?"

"No," he replied, but then he shifted on the stool and winced as muscles cramped along his spine.

"Liar."

He uttered a ragged sigh. "It only bothers me when I'm tense." Which explained why the old injury had been bugging him pretty much ever since Erin Powell had moved to Lakewood and joined the *Chronicle* staff.

"I saw her new column, Powell on Patrol," Paddy said, as if having read his mind. His uncanny intuition was probably what had earned him his promotion to watch commander. "You've got a reason to be tense. She's really out to get you."

"I'm not worried about me." For some reason Kent was worried about *her* and why she was raising her nephew all alone. What had happened to the boy's parents? And had that made Erin the angry woman she was with him?

"No, you're worried about the department," the watch commander surmised. "You're trying to protect it the same way you protected the chief."

Guilt burned through Kent like the alcohol had. "I'm not doing a very good job."

Paddy swiped a cottage fry through the puddle of ketchup on his plate. "Billy told me about your plan."

"*My* plan?" Kent scoffed. "I think it was actually his idea." The younger officer had had to remind Kent that he was still a cop.

"Doesn't matter whose idea as long as you do it," Paddy said. "What have you found out so far about the prickly Erin Powell?"

That she wasn't always prickly.

"Not much," he admitted. "I don't have her date of birth or social security number." If only he'd been able to hack into the *Chronicle*'s employment records, but he upheld the law instead of breaking it. "So I'm having to dig through a lot of Erin Powells to find mine."

"*Yours?*" Paddy raised a brow.

"You all call her that," he replied defensively. "My reporter."

"*We* all call her that," Paddy agreed. "But *you* never have."

Until he'd kissed her tonight.

He shrugged, as if his slip of the tongue meant nothing. "Must have been the tequila talking."

"As long as you weren't talking to her," Paddy muttered, "you're all right."

"What do you mean?" he asked uneasily. Since the watch commander seemed to see everything and know everything, did he know where Kent had been?

"Well, she twists everything you say into something bad," Paddy pointed out matter-of-factly.

"That she does." How would she twist what he'd

done? Would she print details about that kiss? What would his fellow officers say about his fraternizing with the enemy? They wouldn't consider him much of a hero anymore. "So it'd be best for the department—" and himself "—if I stayed away from her."

"Isn't that going to be kind of hard?"

Harder now that he had kissed her. Even if she'd only been messing with his head, she had rattled him. More than he cared to admit.

"You're the public information officer," Paddy pointed out. "It's your job to deal with the media."

Deal with, not kiss.

"Sure," he said, "but I don't need to work with her on anything but press releases and interviews. I'm going to limit my involvement with the CPA."

"But I need you."

"I'll still handle the publicity for the program," Kent promised. "The CPA is a great way to promote community involvement."

Its purpose wasn't, as Erin had claimed, to improve the image of the department. It was to improve the relationship between the department and the community. Paddy had proved, over the past few years, that the effort worked. Kent couldn't let Erin Powell destroy that.

"Not everyone's thrilled about the program," Paddy reminded him.

Kent sighed. "You're talking about Lakewood's esteemed mayor, Joel Standish."

"He'd like to cut it from the budget."

"Among other things," Kent reminded his friend, hoping Paddy wasn't taking the mayor's budget-cutting personally. The blowhard politician was going after the whole department.

"That's probably why his daughter joined the academy—to get ammo for her dad to bring to the city council." Paddy smashed a fry into his plate. "That's why I need you, Kent. I need your help to keep the CPA going."

Kent nodded. "Of course I'll help."

The department and his fellow officers deserved his loyalty. Erin Powell, with her slanderous articles and snarky new column, deserved nothing but his disdain.

To be attracted to her and to give in to that attraction was a betrayal of everything that mattered most to Kent.

Chapter Five

Erin couldn't remember the last time she'd witnessed a woman cooing. Her mother hadn't cooed over Jason when he was a newborn. Maybe a cheerleader in high school had cooed over the quarterback.

That was who the television reporter from Channel 7 reminded Erin of as she fawned over Kent. Erin's face heated with embarrassment for the foolish woman.

"Kent, I'm so sorry I missed the first class," Monica Fox said as she pawed at the sergeant's arm, stroking her red-taloned fingers up and down the sleeve of his black uniform shirt.

Erin barely suppressed a shudder. Maybe she would have to stop showing up early for class. If she'd been late, she might have missed this spectacle in the third-floor conference room of the police department. Kent grinned down at the red-haired woman, his already overinflated ego soaking up all her adoration.

"I know," murmured the college girl as she leaned across the empty chair between her and Erin. "She couldn't be more obvious, could she?"

Amy should know. Erin suspected the only reason the

girl had joined the Citizen's Police Academy was to hook up with a police officer.

Erin couldn't help but agree with the girl, though. "No, she couldn't." And neither could he.

"The important thing is that you're here now," Kent told Monica, flashing the wide grin that Erin had only ever seen on TV.

There was no denying that the camera loved his golden hair, tanned skin and muscular build, but some reporters loved him, too. Was that how he got the good press—by flirting? Was that why he'd tried it with her?

"If there hadn't been that fire on campus..." Monica's finger trailed up his arm to his biceps, tracing it through the material of his uniform "...I would have been here."

"The fire was the big story last week," Kent agreed understandingly. "But I'm so glad you could come tonight." He glanced over to Erin, sitting near the front of the room. "It'll be nice to have some honest coverage of the Citizen's Police Academy."

Monica followed his gaze. "Is she that reporter from the *Chronicle?*"

"Yes, she is," Erin stated wryly.

Monica turned back to Kent, as if she couldn't care less who Erin was. "I wish I could sign up for the class, too, but I have to be available for other news stories."

"I understand," Kent assured her. "The class is filing in, so we should probably get started now so we don't interrupt the lesson for tonight."

Monica giggled—actually *giggled*—then gestured for her camera crew to begin filming.

Teeth clenched, Erin listened to the reporter's pandering interview of the public information officer. Kent gave Monica the same canned spiel he'd given Erin about the CPA building community relations. Monica lapped it up as if every word out of Kent Terlecki's mouth was as rich and irresistible as chocolate mousse.

"I hate chocolate mousse," Erin muttered. "It makes me sick…."

"What?" Amy asked, leaning across the empty seat again. The woman who'd occupied it last week, Tessa Howard, appeared to be late again.

"I just wondered when the class was going to get started," Erin replied.

"Great to see that everyone, or almost everyone, came back for this week's session," Lieutenant O'Donnell said, as he glanced toward that empty chair and then to the emergency vehicle operation expert, Lieutenant Michalski, who sat at the officers' table.

He was the reason Tessa Howard had had to join the class. From what Erin had heard, he had made her a deal: she could join the CPA, or get another speeding violation that would have caused the Secretary of State, Michigan's version of the Department of Motor Vehicles, to suspend her license for having too many points on her driving record. Although Tessa might not agree with the choice, the lieutenant had offered her a way out of a bad situation. So the whole department wasn't as ambitious and self-centered as Kent Terlecki….

His chair sat empty as he followed the reporter and her camera crew into the hall. Erin turned toward the back of the room, to see Tessa rushing in, probably worried that Michalski would change his mind about her ticket if she kept coming to class late.

Lieutenant O'Donnell continued to outline the class program: they would break up into small groups, each with an officer as a guide, to tour the department for the first half.

Was Monica Fox getting a private tour?

KENT SHOVED the reporter's card into his pocket. On her way to the elevator, Monica Fox turned, smiled, then lifted her hand, thumb to her ear, pinkie to her mouth. "Call me," she mouthed.

Kent nodded. He would call her—for media coverage for the department. Nothing else. For the protection and the integrity of the Lakewood PD he could not get involved with *any* reporter.

Especially not Ms. Powell.

Erin met him in the doorway as he tried to reenter the conference room. "Are you all done flirting?" she asked.

He didn't bother denying it; he had flirted a bit—perversely, for her benefit. He'd wanted to make her jealous, which was ridiculous, since she would actually have to be interested in him to get jealous.

"Why are you out here? Were you missing me?" he teased.

She shook her head. "Not hardly. Lieutenant O'Donnell assigned me to your group for the tour."

"Great. Just great." So much for telling Paddy how he needed to avoid her.

"Don't worry," a raspy male voice murmured. "I've got your back, man."

Kent grinned and knocked his knuckles against the tattooed ones of Rafe Sanchez. Rafe bore the tats and the scars from his days in an East Side gang. But he had cleaned up his act back in his teens, and now, a successful businessman, he'd opened a youth center in his old neighborhood in Lakewood. "I'm glad you're in my group, Rafe."

"You're just glad I'm on your side."

From the glance the dark haired man shot at Erin, Kent figured out Rafe wasn't talking about just being on the side of law and order now. He truly had Kent's back.

"You're not doing justice to Sergeant Terlecki," Rafe told Erin, "or the department in your articles. They're not hiding anything from the public. Kent's a good man. The kids down at the youth center like and respect him. And they don't like and respect many people."

Erin smiled. "I appreciate what you're trying to do—"

"These teachers can vouch for how teenagers are," Rafe continued as if she hadn't spoken, including the two women who had just joined their group. Both nodded in agreement.

Kent smiled at the women, who didn't appear much older than the kids they taught at Lakewood Private Academy. "Let's head toward the elevators, and I'll show you around the department."

THE MAN WAS A FLIRT. He probably considered himself charming. Unfortunately, so had the teachers. They hadn't cooed over him like the Channel 7 reporter, but they had been charmed.

Erin snorted in derision. She hadn't been charmed; she'd been ignored during the entire tour, from the parking garage in the basement to the 911 call center on the top floor. Kent hadn't shown them what she'd wanted to see: the evidence lockers and the crime lab. He'd claimed that the public wasn't allowed in those areas.

During the second half of class, the instructors played traffic stop-and-arrest videos, and he still hadn't answered her questions. She'd wanted to know if there were recordings of every incident. If she could find the tape of her brother's arrest, maybe she could finally help him. Kent had answered with some pat response about not everything being a matter of public record. When she'd asked how she could find out what wasn't public, he'd ignored her.

Now, after class had been dismissed, she was being ignored again.

The rest of the CPA participants walked in front of her toward the parking garage, which was a block down and one over from the police department. The weathered brick building sat on a cobblestone street in downtown Lakewood, centrally located near offices, restaurants, the museum and the theater.

Several CPA members hurried toward the warmth of their vehicles as the wind, cool for September, whipped off the nearby lake. Despite the sweater she wore, Erin shivered and hastened her own pace. Her low heels clicked against the sidewalk, nearly masking the soft scrape of the shoes of the person coming up behind her.

Startled, she whirled around, to see a tall, broad-shouldered shadow. Her pulse quickened more with anticipation than fear. Had Kent followed her?

But then the man stepped into the glow of a streetlamp. He wasn't quite as tall or broad as Kent, and his hair had only streaks of blond.

"Reverend Thomas," she murmured to the youth minister who was also a CPA member.

"Call me Holden," he said. "You shouldn't be walking alone out here."

"I'm not alone." She gestured ahead of them, toward the rest of the group, but they had already disappeared around the corner.

"You're all by yourself here," he pointed out. "Despite the police department being close by, this neighborhood can still be dangerous at night. Some street people prey on the after-theater and bar crowd."

"Street people?" She peered into the shadows of the brick buildings, but didn't notice anyone lurking.

"I run a shelter for runaways," he said. "I know that some of them come around here at night, begging and..." he sighed "...doing whatever else they need to to survive."

"I've heard about your shelter." She had wanted to write a feature on it, but her boss had scoffed at her desire to go back to her "bleeding heart" stories. Herb had questioned her desire to be a *real* reporter, and would only allow her to cover the police beat, in addition to the column he'd given her.

"You have?" the reverend asked, as if he doubted anyone had heard of his work.

"You're doing a great job," she assured him, wishing she could say the same about herself. All she could focus on right now, though, was proving her brother's innocence.

"I'm trying." He shook his head. "But it feels really hopeless sometimes."

She glanced at his face as he walked beside her. He probably wasn't much older than her twenty-five years, but fine lines radiated from the corners of his blue-green eyes. "Working with teenagers can be really stressful. My dad's a teacher," she told him.

"Here in Lakewood?" he asked.

"At a private high school in Grand Rapids. He teaches theology." Unfortunately, he didn't always practice what he preached, such as forgiveness. "So I know that teenagers can be really difficult. A lot of people just give up on them." As her dad and mom had given up on Mitchell when he'd gotten a little wild in his teens. They'd been embarrassed, worried about what the school and the church community would think of his antics. "It's wonderful that those kids have a champion like you."

He sighed again. "Like I said, I'm trying, but I definitely understand the term tilting at windmills."

"You need more help." And if Herb Stein would let her run an article on the shelter, she could probably get more help for Reverend Thomas.

"That's why I joined the academy," he admitted.

During the introduction in the first class, last week, all the participants had explained their reasons for joining the academy. Yet she had been too focused on Kent to pay much attention to her classmates.

"Do you want to get some of the other members to volunteer at the shelter?" she asked, her steps slowing as they entered the parking garage. Because she always arrived early, the structure was still filled with the vehicles of people who worked downtown, so she'd had to park on the higher levels.

"That would be great," Holden said as he followed her to the stairwell even though she suspected they'd just passed his vehicle. The midsized SUV was one of the few left in the garage. Unlike Terlecki, Reverend Thomas was a true gentleman, and good-looking with a lean build and beautiful blue-green eyes.

So why did her pulse not quicken as he walked close beside her? Why did she feel no flicker of attraction?

"I'd volunteer myself," she said, "but my young nephew lives with me. Being so busy with work, I already feel as if I don't spend enough time with him."

A muscle twitched in the reverend's cheek, and he nodded. "I understand. My niece lives with me."

Erin sensed there was a story there, maybe one similar to hers, but she didn't want to pry. She hated it when people asked too many questions about why Jason lived with her.

"Who I'd really like to have help out with the shelter," Holden said, "are members of the police department."

"They don't?"

"Their idea—or at least *one* officer's idea—of help is to arrest my kids." Frustration furrowed his brow and vibrated in his voice. "She—they—don't understand how that destroys instead of builds trust."

"I understand." Erin worried that Jason might never get over his own fear of police officers.

She opened the door to the level on which she'd parked, and Holden Thomas followed her out. Her tan minivan was the only vehicle left, so she'd been right: he was the gentleman she'd thought him.

The wind whipped over the concrete barriers, ruffling his hair and blowing hers across her face. "Thank you for walking with me," she said.

Holden nodded, then commented, "I read your column, Ms. Powell."

Was that why he'd caught up with her? Someone besides Herb Stein actually appreciated what she wrote?

"I don't agree with you," he said. "While I wish the police department would do more to help out at the shelter, I understand that everyone's busy. They're understaffed and overworked. I appreciate how difficult their job is, but they do their duty protecting and serving Lakewood."

Erin wondered if he didn't appreciate that *one* officer more than the others. Or perhaps less. That was her problem, too, really, just one officer.

BILLY HALLIDAY SLAPPED his palm onto the suddenly vacated stool next to him at the bar. "Hey, roomie, have a seat."

For once Kent wasn't annoyed that someone had given up a stool for him. After today's class, and fielding all of Erin's questions, exhaustion tugged at his muscles and his mind.

"Hey, man," Kent replied. "Haven't seen much of you lately."

"Yeah, I've been deep."

"I thought you were just laying low to avoid your mom," Kent teased, glancing over his shoulder to where Marla Halliday sat with the other CPA participants. "But then you wouldn't have showed up here."

"Not if I wanted to avoid her," Billy agreed with a sigh. But he didn't even glance toward his mother. His focus remained on the auburn-haired woman behind the bar. Brigitte Kowalczek, granddaughter of the man who owned the Lighthouse, had enrolled in the CPA, but Kent hadn't quite figured out why. She spent a lot of time with police officers at the bar and had never seemed interested in them beyond getting their drinks. Billy, however, tracked her every move.

Brigitte and Billy?

Hell, Kent guessed it made more sense than him and Erin. *That* made no sense at all.

"What's this?" Billy asked, leaning over to pick something out of the peanut shells on the floor.

Kent recognized the Channel 7 logo in the corner of the card and patted his now-empty pocket. He hadn't bothered changing out of his uniform before coming to the bar. Since he never knew when he might need to talk to the press, he kept a uniform at home, too. "That's Monica Fox's card."

Billy lifted a dark brow. "Oh? And why would you be carrying *her* card around?"

"Nah, it's not like that." Kent knew how his friend's mind worked. "It's only business."

Billy laughed as he flipped over the card. "That's why she wrote her private cell number on the back under the words *Call me.*"

"That's not what you think," Kent said, even though he wasn't naive enough to believe it wasn't. Monica had made her interest in him pretty clear, and apparently he wasn't the only one who'd figured it out.

"I think you should give her a call," Billy suggested as he passed the card back to Kent.

He shoved it in his pocket, shaking his head. "That wouldn't be a good idea."

"This chick has been after you for a while," Billy reminded him. "When are you going to stop playing hard to get?"

Kent grinned. "I'm not hard to get."

Not if the woman drew his interest, like Erin Powell did. If she didn't hate him, he would have been easy for her to get.

"So you're just playing?" Billy teased. "My roommate, the '*playa.*'"

"Yeah, that's me," Kent scoffed. He knew his friend, who usually called him a boring old man, was only kidding. Apparently Erin Powell didn't, though. She gasped, drawing their attention to where she stood behind them, unabashedly eavesdropping.

"Erin—"

She whirled and returned to the table with the rest of the CPA members, but she didn't sit back down. Instead, she grabbed up her purse and headed toward the door.

Kent slid off his stool, but a strong hand on his arm held him back from following her.

"Let her go," Billy advised. "Goodbye and good riddance when it comes to that woman, Bullet. She's nothing but trouble for you."

She was more than that. He had finally worked his way through the list of Erin Powells and found *his.* She hadn't always been the bitter woman she was now, but he hadn't found out yet what had made her so hateful.

"I need to talk to her," Kent insisted.

"You need to wring her neck," Billy muttered, turning back toward the bar—and the bartender. He didn't even notice Kent's wave as he headed after Erin.

Kent followed her out the door and through the dimly lit parking lot. She moved fast, so he didn't catch her until she was about to climb into her minivan. That first night she had followed him to the Lighthouse, he'd thought her choice of vehicle strange for a single woman. Now he understood.

She whirled toward him, a can of pepper spray directed toward his face. Obviously she'd heard his approach. Was there anything the woman missed—beside the fact that he was really a nice guy? Pride and respect that she could take care of herself flashed through him.

He held up his hands. "I'd say don't shoot, but now that you know it's me, you're certain to."

"I'm not going to shoot—or spray—you," she said, and dropped the canister back in her purse.

"You're sure?" he asked. "You seem pretty upset by whatever you overheard." He couldn't believe he hadn't noticed her behind him. He'd been out of the field for only three years, but his instincts must have grown dull. Would he be able to go back if he ever got the bullet out?

"I don't know what you're talking about," she stated. "I wasn't eavesdropping."

"Yes, you were," he insisted. "If that's how you do your *investigative* reporting, it's no wonder you get everything wrong in your articles."

Maybe he should ask her for some pointers, because even though he'd learned more about her, he hadn't yet discovered why she hated him.

"I don't get anything wrong," she argued. "I've been right about you all along."

He sighed. "Erin, you have no idea—"

"And now I know how you're getting some good press," she exclaimed, her voice sharp with anger. "You're sleeping with reporters."

Kent, intrigued by the trace of jealousy he detected on her beautiful face, stepped close, trapping her between the open door of her van and his body. "Don't you wish…"

Chapter Six

Regrettably, she did wish. It must have been because she hadn't had a relationship in so long that she was even remotely attracted to Kent Terlecki. Face flaming, she ducked her head to glance at her watch, but couldn't even read the dial. His broad shoulders blocked the faint glow of the parking lot lamp. Her pulse raced at his closeness, at the heat of his body chasing the chill from hers.

"I have to go…."

"What are you now?" Kent asked, his voice deep with amusement and that potent charm. "Cinderella?"

"I'm late. I have to get home to Jason." Before her mother got so mad that she refused to watch him anymore. Oh, heck, Erin was probably already too late not to make her mother mad. If her mom stopped babysitting, Erin would have to quit the CPA. There was no one else Jason was comfortable enough to stay with without his nerves and separation anxiety bringing on an asthma attack.

And if she left the CPA, she would lose the column Herb had given her, and probably her job, as well. Since the *Chronicle* was the only newspaper in Lakewood, she didn't have any other employment options. How would she take care of Jason then?

"I really have to go," she said, hoping she could sweet-talk her mother into giving her another chance. She tried to ease past him to slide onto the driver's seat, but instead of giving her room, he stepped even closer and put his hand on her shoulder.

"Do you have time for a question?" he asked.

"No." Her skin tingled beneath the warmth of his palm. She tried shrugging it off, but his grip tightened.

"I'll answer one of yours if you answer mine," he offered.

Would she finally learn the reason for his nickname? Or should she pose the question that was most important to her: had he framed her brother to boost his arrest record? No, she would have to know him better before she dared ask that. There was no point in asking a question if you knew the person was only going to lie.

"Okay," she agreed. Her chance of cajoling her mother was not very good anyway. She and her brother had never been able to talk her into or out of anything.

"What's your question for me?" she asked, betting that it was about Jason and how she had come to be his guardian. She didn't intend to tell Terlecki the truth; she had shared with very few people where her brother actually was.

But as Kent leaned in, his head dipping close to hers, she worried that he was going to ask her for another kiss. And that she would be helpless to say anything but yes. She held her breath, willing herself to resist him.

His gray eyes glinted under the streetlamp, and his

lips curved into a slight grin. "How does an idealist turn into a tabloid reporter?"

Defensive and oddly disappointed, she bristled. "The *Chronicle* is not a tabloid."

"It's not a legit paper, either."

"Of course it is. We print all the news in the Lakewood area." Except those stories that Herb considered bleeding-heart pieces, like Reverend Thomas's shelter for runaways.

Kent's chuckle was more patronizing than amused. "You only print the news that the mayor wants covered."

"That's crazy," she scoffed, shaking her head in disbelief.

"Everyone knows that Mayor Standish owns Herb Stein and a controlling interest in the *Chronicle,*" he informed her. "Joel Standish uses the paper to push his own agenda."

She hadn't lived in Lakewood long enough to understand the city's politics. "I don't get what any of that has to do with me."

"Haven't you wondered why, after barely a year of working for the *Chronicle,* you've been given your own column?"

She had, but she wouldn't admit that to him. "Because I'm a good reporter."

He laughed. "Because you're writing what the mayor wants you to write."

"I haven't even met the mayor," she said.

"He's still your boss, and he's using you, Erin." Kent sounded concerned, as if he actually cared about her. "The mayor has it in for the chief, and he's using you to help him discredit the department."

She tensed, wishing she could ease away from him, but the door at her back trapped her, their bodies so close that his badge nearly brushed her sweater. He was flirting with her, she reminded herself, just as he flirted with every other woman who crossed his path.

"Of course you would say that," she said, "because I'm not letting *you* use me like Monica Fox does."

He leaned forward so that his face nearly touched Erin's. "Nothing's going on with me and Monica Fox."

A breath of relief eased the pressure in her lungs. She shouldn't care if he was sleeping with the gorgeous television reporter. She shouldn't care at all about his personal life. And he shouldn't care about hers. "Why did you ask me that question? What do you mean about my being an idealist?"

"I know about the Peace Corps," he said. "How you entered it right out of college. I read the articles you wrote while you were in South America."

She swallowed, nerves and emotion threatening to choke her. "You did?"

"They were good," he declared, "inspiring even. They're a far cry from what you've written about me and the Lakewood PD."

"I was a different person back then." Before she had found out about her brother's arrest. Her parents had kept it from her while she was in the Corps. They hadn't wanted to distract her from the work she'd been doing. And they hadn't thought she could do anything to help her brother.

She hoped they were wrong.

"I think you're still that person," Kent said. His hand squeezed her shoulder. "Inside."

Her pulse leaped, but she didn't shrug off his touch. "You don't know me, and no matter how much digging you do, you're never going to know me," she said, trying to convince herself, as well as him.

"I would if you'd let me in," he murmured. His fingers moved up to her neck and the curve of her jaw.

She needed to slap his hand away. She needed to shove him back, but all she could do was stare into his face, handsome even in the dim light of the parking lot. She'd dated in high school and college, but none of those men had made her heart pound this hard. *Why him?*

"I need to go," she said, wincing when she realized she sounded as if she was asking his permission. "I need to get home…to Jason…."

Kent nodded as if he understood, but he didn't step back. He moved closer still, so that their bodies touched—thighs rubbing against thighs, breasts against chest. His hand slid up her to cup her cheek, and he lowered his head.

Erin flicked her tongue across her lower lip in anticipation of his kiss, but his mouth didn't touch hers.

His lips only brushed across her cheek, his breath tickling her ear as he asked, "What about your question for me, Erin?"

"I—I…" She had so many questions she wanted to ask him. Such as when was he going to kiss her….

"What do you want to know about me?" he asked, his voice a low, sexy rasp.

Erin shivered despite the warmth of his body pressed against hers. She shook her head, resisting temptation. "I can't…"

She could not be attracted to him—any man but Kent Terlecki.

"Can't?" he prompted.

"I don't have time to..." She swallowed hard, fighting the desire that tempted her to close the distance between their mouths. "I don't have time to interview you."

He drew back slightly, enough that she could see the curve of his lips. "I didn't agree to an interview, Ms. Powell. Just one question."

"I can't...not tonight." The question would have to wait.

He studied her face, but she assured herself that he couldn't see the need in her eyes in the dim light. *She hoped.*

Finally he stepped back. "Then another night."

Her pulse kept tripping along. Another night. Would he kiss her then as he had before? No, he couldn't—and she couldn't want him to.

She slid under the steering wheel, but before she closed the door, she said, "Remember that when I do ask you that question, you owe me an *honest* answer."

"I promise," he said. "I've never been anything but honest with you."

She refrained from calling him a liar, because she had no proof, but she reminded him, "You've been evasive."

"I won't evade this question. I'm giving you a freebie, Ms. Powell."

"I will collect," she vowed as she closed the door. Her hand shook as she turned the key in the ignition. She wanted to collect more than that answer. She wanted another kiss.

"HOW ABOUT GIVING ME THAT honest answer?"

Kent jumped, surprised that he was no longer alone. But his attention had been focused on the taillights of Erin's van as she pulled out of the lot. He should be glad she'd left before he'd done something stupid—like kiss her again.

But his tense body and pounding heart protested his restraint. He almost believed that she'd wanted him to, that she'd waited for his kiss. For the first time Kent cursed his control.

He turned in the direction of the familiar voice. Billy stepped from the shadows.

Kent used to be as stealthy as his friend, but after spending the past three years on the evening news, he would probably never be able to go undercover again.

"What do you want an honest answer about?" he finally asked.

"How you really feel about Erin Powell?" Billy's dark eyes were intent on his face.

Kent edged back a few feet, afraid of betraying his true feelings. Knowing what his friend expected him to say, he replied, "She's a pain in the ass."

"But you like her," Sergeant Halliday stated, as if accusing Kent of a crime.

He shrugged. "She hates my guts."

But she hadn't pushed him away or kneed him in the groin. Maybe she didn't hate him as much as she wanted to. Why did she *want* to hate him? He still hadn't found out the reason.

Billy snorted. "You don't hate hers."

"I don't hate her," he admitted, "but I wouldn't say I *like* her." He wanted her, though. He wanted all the passion she revealed in her column and that he'd seen in those old articles he'd found. Erin Powell might have lost her idealism, but she hadn't lost her fire.

"She's certainly given you no reason to like her," Billy reminded him. "God, man, we can't have all that bad press right now. You know that better than anyone else."

Kent sighed. "Yeah, Mayor Standish is breathing down the chief's neck." Probably because Frank Archer was the only man the mayor couldn't buy, manipulate or bully. But the chief was too popular with the city council and the public for the mayor to simply fire him. So he was punishing him another way. Kent couldn't help but think it was personal; the two men had known each other a long time. "Standish is looking for any reason to cut our budget."

"And Erin Powell is giving him the ammunition with every column she writes."

Kent groaned, the last of his desire for her draining from his body. "I'm trying to do something about that," he insisted. "I'm trying to find out more about her."

"So you can neutralize her, or because you're interested in her?" Billy asked.

"I'm not..." He couldn't lie to his best friend. He couldn't deny Erin intrigued him...and attracted him. He'd always loved a mystery, but everything he learned about her just raised more questions...and his interest in her.

Billy sighed. "You're not going to call the Channel 7 lady, are you?"

"No, I'm not going to call her." He reached into his pocket for the reporter's card and handed it to his friend. "But you can."

Billy passed it back. "No."

"Why not?"

"She's interested in you, not me." He gestured toward his beard and shaggy hair.

Kent narrowed his eyes, catching a hint of something else in his friend's tone. "And you're interested in someone else."

Billy shook his head. "No, that's not it. You know how vice is, man. I don't have time for anyone or anything in my life but the job."

Kent remembered how it was, but unlike all the other times he'd thought about that life, he didn't miss it. Instead he stared off in the direction Erin's van had driven. He missed *her.* If only they were different people and he could pursue this attraction…

But even if she didn't hate him, Kent still had a bullet in his back—one that could eventually cause nerve damage or paralysis. It was better that she hate him, better that they stay uninvolved, than for her to have someone else she would have to take care of.

Chapter Seven

"I've been waiting for this column," Herb Stein grumbled as Erin passed the hard copy across his desk.

She had given him one version already, but he'd tossed it back at her, demanding that she add more "bite." Was Kent right? Was she being used to push the mayor's agenda?

"I'm sorry, sir," she said, "I really don't understand what was wrong with the first version." In it, she had focused on the videos the police instructors had shown after the tour of the department at the second class. If only there'd been footage of Mitchell's arrest. Still, she was compelled to admit, "Those videos were quite interesting and enlightening."

Like Reverend Thomas, Erin was actually beginning to understand and appreciate the challenge of being a police officer. The other officers she'd met during the first two weeks of the CPA were not like Kent Terlecki, ruthlessly ambitious to get ahead in the department. Lieutenant Michalski and the watch commander especially seemed to care genuinely about protecting and serving the community. They reminded her of why she had joined the Peace Corps, because she'd felt as though it had been her calling. Deciding to become a police officer, to put oneself in that kind of danger, had to be a calling, too.

She hoped to learn more about the job during the ride-along she'd signed up for, where she would actually accompany an officer during his or her shift. But she was beginning to doubt that the editor-in-chief would let her use much, if any, of what she learned in her column. She resisted the urge, barely, to point out that Powell on Patrol was supposed to be about her adventures in the CPA.

"The first version didn't have the same tone of your other articles," Herb explained.

"It did where I mentioned Sergeant Terlecki," she reminded him.

"Yeah." Herb slapped the paper. "This is it. *He* was what you needed to focus on."

She had tried to write about something else pertaining to the department because she focused on Kent entirely too much. She couldn't get him out of her head. But she had more important things—more important people—to worry about.

She glanced at her watch. "So is the column all right now?"

"Yeah, yeah…" A grin split the older man's jowly face. "This is great. You got the tone exactly right now."

She doubted Kent would be as thrilled about that as her boss was. "Can I leave a little early then?"

"Sure." He shrugged. "You've been working Wednesday nights, taking the classes. You can have this afternoon off."

A sigh of relief eased the pressure in her chest. Maybe she could pick up Jason before the assembly started, which his teacher had warned Erin might upset him.

"Thank you," she murmured as she hurried out of his office.

Traffic between downtown and Jason's school in the suburbs slowed her progress and, regrettably, gave her time to think. As always, when that happened, she thought about *him.*

She should have asked Kent the question the other night—the one he had promised to answer honestly. He'd given her a free shot, but she hadn't taken it. What was wrong with her?

As usual she hadn't had time. She'd barely managed to convince her mother to keep babysitting on Wednesday nights. Thankfully, Kathryn had understood that if Erin lost her job, she'd have trouble supporting herself and Jason.

She breathed another sigh of relief as she drove up to the elementary school. Instead of finding a parking space in the crowded lot, she pulled to the curb and vaulted out of the van, worried about Jason. The speaker at the school assembly was a police officer.

As she rushed inside, she checked her purse, making sure she had his inhaler in case the one Jason took to school was empty. The secretary jumped up from her desk inside the glass walls of her office. Recognizing Erin, she smiled and pointed down the hall toward the gymnasium.

Erin was at the school entirely too often. On her own, she wasn't enough to make Jason feel secure and confident. He needed a man in his life so that he wouldn't panic every time someone spoke much above a whisper.

She slowed her steps as she neared the gym. Although she strained to listen, she could hear only the deep murmur of a male voice, no giggling or squabbling children. In fact, she couldn't remember the last time she had heard the school so quiet.

Careful not to disturb anyone, she slowly pushed open the swinging doors and stepped inside the gym. The kids, sitting cross-legged on the floor, stared—some open mouthed—at the man standing in front of them. Erin turned toward him and her mouth fell open, too.

"I know," murmured Mrs. Moskett as she joined Erin. "He's gorgeous, isn't he? Almost tempts me to break a law."

Erin forced a smile. While she couldn't agree with Jason's teacher, she couldn't argue with her, either. Kent Terlecki's broad shoulders and muscular chest filled out the Lakewood Police Department's black uniform pulse-racingly well.

"'Course, I don't think my husband would understand," the older woman continued. "But I'm sure you can." Color rushed to the teacher's face. "O-Oh, that's right. You…he…the articles you write…"

"How is Jason doing?" Erin asked, trying to find her nephew in the mass of little bodies crowding the floor of the sun-filled gymnasium.

"Very well," Mrs. Moskett said with relief. "He recognized Sergeant Terlecki as your 'friend' so he didn't panic."

Mrs. Moskett was one of the few people who knew the truth about where Jason's father was. She didn't know, however, that Sergeant Kent Terlecki was the one who'd put him there. And neither must Jason as he stared up at him, as enthralled as all the other kids. Kent spoke about an officer's job, about an officer's sworn duty to protect and serve the community, but he brought it down to their level, explaining it so they understood and were entertained.

And despite herself, so was Erin.

PLASTERING A GRIN on his face, Kent braced himself and asked, "Does anyone have any questions for me?"

Little hands lifted as if they were doing the wave at a football game. High-pitched voices called out, "Me! Me!"

He pointed toward a little girl with pale blond braids and big blue eyes who sat in the front row. Surely *she* wouldn't ask *that* question. "What would you like to know, honey?"

Her voice soft and quaking with nerves, she asked, "Have you ever shot someone?"

With effort Kent hung on to his smile. "An officer only discharges his weapon when he has no other choice," he explained, "and he has to protect him or herself or other innocent people."

He didn't hear her actually snort, but some noise drew his attention to where Erin stood by the doors to the gymnasium. Was she following him now? Even from a distance, he noticed the arch of her dark brow. *Other* innocent people? He instinctively knew that was the comment to which she'd taken exception. While he wasn't the bad guy she'd like everyone to think he was, he wasn't exactly guilt-free, either, not with the thoughts, the *dreams,* he'd been having about her lately.

In his dreams, she didn't mind him being bad. In fact, she liked it. *A lot.* His grin widened.

Until a boy, too impatient to wait until Kent called on him, shouted out, "Have you ever killed someone?"

Kent closed his eyes, but saw the face of another kid much older in years and experience than the young faces staring up at him. The usual mantra rang through Kent's head: *I had no choice...it was him or me...*

But that mantra hadn't eased his guilt all those years ago when he'd exchanged gunfire with the gang member.

"Sergeant Terklecki?" the little boy who'd asked the question prodded. "Have you killed somebody?"

"Very rarely does an officer have to take a life in the line of duty." Thank God. "And Lakewood is a very safe community." Yet like any community, there was crime—more crime than the department would be able to handle if their budget got cut any more.

The principal, a Mary Poppins type with a squeaky high voice and perpetual smile, stepped up beside him. To save him? "We only have time for one more question for public information officer Sergeant Terlecki," she said, "Then we have to get back to our rooms and collect our things, because the bell will ring soon."

Almost done.

"So who has another question for our wonderful guest?" the principal asked. She pointed toward a little dark-haired boy whom Kent should have noticed earlier.

Color fled the kid's face, leaving him pale, his eyes stark behind his thick-lensed glasses. The boy was smaller and frailer in appearance than the children sitting around him, and now he looked sick.

"Hey, Jason," Kent said in greeting, recognizing Erin's nephew even though the kid hadn't had on his glasses the other night. "What's your question, buddy?"

The boy's schoolmates turned to him, obviously awed that Jason knew a police officer. Jason lifted his chin a bit, as if he was proud to be recognized, and bravely asked, "Do only bad people have to go to jail?"

Kent wanted to glance at Erin, to gauge her reaction to her nephew's question, but for some reason he didn't dare break eye contact with the kid. This question was important to Jason. So Kent answered him truthfully. "No. Not everyone in jail is a bad person."

"Then why do they go to jail if they're not bad?" another kid piped up.

Kent continued to hold Jason's gaze. The boy hadn't blinked, his dark eyes watchful as he waited for Kent's answer.

"There are bad people in jail," he clarified. Jason flinched. "But there are good people in jail, too. They just made a pretty bad mistake to wind up there."

Or someone else had, Erin thought. *Someone like him.* Her brother, Jason's father, was not a criminal. Kent had to have made a mistake.

The principal urged the kids to stand up and clap in appreciation for Kent coming to speak to them. The children didn't just clap. They stomped and stampeded, rushing to where Kent stood at the front of the room. Tall as he was, they barely came to his waist, so he crouched to their level. One little girl wrapped her arms around his neck, clinging to him. He lifted her, but despite her slight weight, a grimace of pain distorted his handsome face. Erin winced herself, sympathizing with him.

She felt compelled to wade through the children to his side, but by the time she got there, Principal Andersen had already pried the little girl from his arms and shooed the kids from the gym.

Erin suddenly stood alone with Kent.

"Apparently I'm not the only one who asks you tough questions," she remarked. Jason's question had stunned her, leaving her frozen and helpless to do anything but listen to Kent's reply and hope that his answer didn't crush the sweet little boy.

As Kent turned to her, looking away from the children filing out, the grin left his face. "No, you're not."

She ignored the twinge of disappointment she felt that he didn't bother smiling at her. She wanted to thank him for answering Jason the way he had, but then he might ask why the boy had asked such a question in the first place.

She cleared her throat and said, "I didn't know you did school assemblies."

He nodded. "Part of my job description."

"That's the only reason you're here?" she asked, studying him through narrowed eyes.

"Yeah, it might not be my favorite part of the job, but it's an important part," he said. "Kids have to know they can trust police officers, that we're here to help them."

She would never be able to trust him. "You didn't come to Maple Valley Elementary because you knew this was where Jason goes to school?"

"Why would you think I knew that?"

"Because you've been checking into my background," she reminded him. She wasn't comfortable that he had learned about her work in the Peace Corps—that he knew who she'd once been. "What you're doing could be considered police harassment, Sergeant."

"When *you* do it, it's considered freedom of the press," he said.

She couldn't fight the smile from lifting her lips. "Of course."

"So when are you asking *your* question?"

"When I can be sure you'll answer me honestly."

"You better not wait too long to figure that out," he warned her. "I just might put an expiration date on that offer."

"Sergeant Terlecki," Principal Andersen called from the busy hallway. "I have some cards for you that the kids made to show their appreciation for your coming today."

"That's really nice," Kent replied, walking away without so much as a backward glance.

"Jason's waiting for you at the office," Mrs. Andersen said to Erin.

She nodded and followed them out of the gym, listening to Mrs. Andersen fawn over Kent in nearly the same nauseating manner that Monica Fox had. At least the principal didn't want to sleep with him, probably not even in her dreams. Erin doubted the perky administrator's dreams ever went beyond a G rating.

If only Erin could say the same…

"Hey, Jase," she greeted her nephew. She didn't have to force a smile for him. "I'm so proud of you." Knowing that the first grader sometimes carried some surprisingly heavy books home, she reached out to lift the backpack from his bony shoulders.

But Jason stepped away and shook his head. "I got it, Aunt E." His skinny arms straining, he pushed through the heavy steel doors and stepped into the sunshine.

"You were so brave," she praised him as they walked down the sidewalk to where she had parked the van at the curb.

He shrugged. "I wasn't afraid, because Sarge is your friend."

Obviously, Jason remembered only the part of Kent's name that he'd managed to utter before Erin had interrupted him. She hadn't wanted him to introduce himself as a police officer for fear of scaring the boy more than he'd already been.

"Ah…" She couldn't deny the friendship and confuse him. She popped the lock and pushed open the sliding side door. "Yes, he is. You shouldn't be afraid of him or any other officers."

Had she told him that enough or had she been so caught up in her own bitterness and anger that she hadn't helped her nephew overcome his fear? She closed her eyes, feeling a wave of shame.

The little boy drew in a shaky breath but denied his fear. "I'm not 'fraid of police officers," he insisted.

"That's good." After getting him settled, she double-checked the seat belt and the booster chair he was required to use because of his small size. She'd promised her brother she would keep his son safe. She used to lie awake nights worrying that she'd fail them both.

She stepped back and bumped into a hard male body. A strong hand closed over her shoulder. "Easy there," Kent cautioned, his breath warm in her ear and against her throat.

Now she lay awake nights thinking about Kent. She shivered and tried to ease away, but his grip tightened. He leaned in to peer inside the van.

"Hey, buddy," he said, "that was a great question you asked me."

"Hey, Aunt E.," Jason said, drawing her attention back to him, "since Sarge is your friend, how come he never comes over for dinner?"

"Uh—uh…" she stammered, at a complete loss for words.

But Kent wasn't. "Yes, Aunt E., how come you never have me over for dinner?"

"Can you come tonight?" Jason asked.

He grinned. "I'm not busy tonight. And I am really hungry."

"Me, too," the little boy said with a big grin at his new idol. Then he turned to Erin. "Can he come over, Aunt E.?"

"Yes, can I?" Kent asked, his gray eyes twinkling.

Erin chewed the inside of her lip, swallowing the response she really wanted to make.

"P-please," Jason beseeched her, his big eyes bright and hopeful behind his thick lenses.

Erin couldn't crush that hope—especially not over Kent Terlecki. "Sure…"

"Guess who's coming to dinner," Kent said with a wicked smile. "I have to stop back at the department, but I'll meet the two of you at home."

At home. He'd said it as if her place was his home, too. And she didn't correct him; she only watched as he walked to his police cruiser and slid behind the wheel. He was coming *home*…with them, as if they were a family.

Jason deserved a family to replace the one he'd lost, but Kent Terlecki could never be part of it.

Chapter Eight

Kent swiped his last chicken nugget through the puddle of ketchup on his plate. He couldn't remember the last time he had eaten a chicken nugget, probably not since college.

"Do you want the rest of mine?" Jason generously offered, pushing his SpongeBob plate with most of his untouched dinner toward Kent.

"No," Erin answered for him. "You need to eat all your food, young man, if you're going to grow up big and strong."

Their table, shoved into a corner of the living room next to the galley kitchen, was so small that Kent's knee rubbed against Erin's. Sure, he could have moved a little closer to Jason, but he kind of liked rubbing up against her. Of course, his body tensed with every contact.

"He's big and strong already," Kent said.

Jason giggled and pushed his glasses up his nose. "No, I'm not. I'm the littlest one in my class."

"So was I when I was your age," Kent assured him.

Behind his lenses, Jason's dark eyes goggled. "You were?"

"Really?" Erin asked, as ever, doubting that he spoke the truth.

"Really," he vowed. "I wasn't just little, though. I was *puny.* And I had asthma—"

"I have asthma!" Jason exclaimed.

"Yeah, that's not fun," Kent sympathized, "especially when I lived on the farm."

"You lived on a farm?" the little boy asked, nearly as fascinated by that as most kids were over Kent's being a police officer.

He nodded. "Up north. It was a cherry farm. Still is, I guess."

"You haven't been up there in a while?" Erin asked.

He shook his head. "Nah…"

He hadn't talked to his family since he'd decided to join the police academy instead of coming home to the farm after college graduation.

"Do you still have asthma?" Jason asked.

"I outgrew it."

"Will I outgrow it?" he asked hopefully.

"Maybe—if you eat all your food and get big and strong," Erin advised him.

"Like Sarge," Jason said around a mouthful of nugget as he gobbled down the ones he'd had left. Then he shoved in his last few spoonfuls of macaroni and cheese.

"Go wash up," Erin told him when he finished.

The little boy vaulted out of his chair and ran off down the hall, leaving his aunt and Kent alone at that intimately small table. But with as much speed as her nephew, Erin jumped up from her seat and gathered up the plates.

"Thanks for dinner," he said as he followed her into the narrow kitchen, where she piled the dishes in the sink.

"Nuggets and mac and cheese." She turned toward him with a smirk. "Aren't you glad you invited yourself over?"

"Jason invited me," he reminded her. "He's a great kid, Erin."

"Yeah, he is."

"That was an interesting question he asked me during the assembly."

She turned back to the sink and reached for the faucet. "It was?"

Kent leaned closer so she would hear him over the noise of the running water. "Usually the only kids who ask me that question know someone who's in jail." Was it one or both of Jason's parents? Was that why he lived with his aunt?

Kent intended to ask her, but the delicate curve of her jaw and throat distracted him. She was so damn beautiful. He reached out and pushed a strand of silky, chocolate-brown hair behind her ear, as he had watched her do a million times in the past year.

"Don't touch me," she murmured, closing her eyes.

"Do you hate me that much," he asked, "that my touch repulses you?"

"I wish it did," she said. "God, I wish it did…."

She turned and ended up stepping into the arms he'd braced on the counter on either side of her. She lifted her palms as if she intended to push him away, but like the other night, her hands lingered. The warmth of her skin penetrated the thin cotton T-shirt he'd changed into when he'd gone back to the department.

"Your touch doesn't repulse me, either," he admitted.

"It should." She sighed. "It should…."

"Because of the things you write about me, twisting

my words to make it look like I'm an idiot who doesn't deserve my job?" he said. "Yeah, it should."

He reached up and cupped her face. "But when I get close to you, all I want to do is this…" He brushed his mouth across hers.

She clutched at his shirt as she kissed him back, slanting her mouth under his, opening her lips so that he could deepen the kiss. She might not have offered much for dinner, but dessert was more than he could have hoped for.

The control that had kept him from kissing her in the parking lot was gone. He lifted her onto the edge of the sink and rocked her hips against where he ached for her. She moaned low in her throat and wrapped her long legs around his waist, arching into him.

Her breasts pushed against his chest. He wanted to touch them, and slid his hands under her shirt and over the thin lace of her bra. Her nipples hardened and pressed against his palms. She murmured again, her tongue slipping between his lips, tangling with his.

The sound of little feet pounding against the hardwood floor brought Kent quickly to his senses. He pulled back even as Erin clung to him, kissing him with all the passion he'd always suspected her capable of.

"Erin…"

She blinked and stared up at him as if she'd forgotten who they both were. Then her eyes widened in shock and she scrambled off the edge of the sink. Water spilled from the still-running faucet, onto the floor. "Oh…"

Kent reached around her to shut off the faucet, and couldn't help but whistle over the way the wet denim clung to the curves of her butt.

Jason joined them in the small kitchen, pushing between them to grasp Kent's hand. "Aunt E.," he said, taking in her wet jeans and the puddle on the floor. He lowered his voice to a whisper. "Did you have an *accident?*"

With her gaze locked on Kent, she nodded miserably. "Yes. Yes, I had an accident."

"She left the sink running," Kent explained as she grabbed paper towels and soaked up the mess. "Let's help your aunt clean up."

"I've got it under control," she assured him.

Now. But a little while ago he was sure she'd been ready to make love with him. If only Jason hadn't come running…

Kent expelled a ragged breath. He should be relieved that the kid had interrupted them. He couldn't get in any deeper with Erin. She couldn't be trusted.

"I wanna show you my room," the boy said, tugging on Kent's hand.

Clearing his throat, and pushing away the desire that had nearly strangled him, he reminded the child, "I've seen your room before."

"But you haven't seen my toys," Jason pointed out. "Come play with me."

Erin shook her head. "Not tonight, Jason. You have homework."

"Oh, Aunt E., all I have to do is read to you," the boy said. "I can read to Sarge instead."

She shook her head again, her delicate jaw clenched. "No, Sergeant Terlecki has to leave now."

"He can't play with me?" Jason asked, his voice rising almost in a whine.

"No, he can't." She turned to Kent, and her eyes finished what she left unsaid. *He can't play with me, either.*

Kent nodded. She was right. Because playing with her was playing with fire—and she had already burned him too many times.

HER MOUTH DRY WITH NERVES, Erin settled onto the plastic seat, facing the tempered glass where she could see her brother when they brought him in from his cell. She always worried about what condition she would find him in—hurt from a fight, worn-out from lack of sleep or emaciated because he hadn't been eating.

She hated that he was in here, and she used to hate the man who had put him behind bars. Unfortunately, she couldn't quite bring herself to hate Kent anymore, no matter how much she still wanted to.

She sat up as a guard led Mitchell into the room on the other side of the glass. Dark circles rimmed his eyes and he barely managed a smile as he settled onto the chair across from her. Hand trembling, Erin reached for the phone, but she couldn't meet his gaze. After kissing Kent, not once but twice, she couldn't face her brother. Yet she'd been compelled to come see him, to talk to him.

"Erin, what's going on?" Mitchell's voice emanated from the receiver she'd pressed to her ear. "Is Jason okay?"

"Yes," she assured him. "He's fine." Ecstatic actually, since Kent had admitted to being small for his age and asthmatic himself as a child.

A sigh of relief rattled the phone. "You scared me for a minute."

"I'm sorry." She closed her eyes at the threat of tears burning behind her lids.

"Sheesh, Erin, what's going on?" he asked. "You're acting like Mom."

"What do you mean?"

"You can't even look at me."

She forced herself to meet his gaze through the glass. "Everything's fine."

Another sigh rattled in her ear. "Good. I don't know what I'd do without you, kid. You're the only one who believes in me. Your articles have kept me going in here." He chuckled. "And I love your column. Powell on Patrol. Your latest one might be my favorite."

Instead of feeling pride at her older brother's praise, she thought of Kent and what would certainly be his disapproval. And maybe hurt. But she'd written it before the other night, before he'd charmed her nephew—and *her*—at their apartment. If not for Jason's presence, Kent probably would have *charmed* her right into bed.

"Jason's doing well," she stated.

"Good," her brother said again. "So tell me what's going on with my son."

"How about I bring him to see you and he tells you what's been going on in his life?"

Mitchell shook his head. "I don't want him here, Erin. You know that."

"But he hasn't seen you in so long." She should have ignored her brother's wishes and brought Jason anyway.

"That's good. The less he sees of me, the less he'll think about me and the less he'll miss me. I'm going to be in here a few more years…" His throat moved as he swallowed hard.

"That's why Jason should come see you."

"No." His voice vibrated in the phone with vehemence.

"But he needs a man in his life."

"So get him a man, sis." Mitchell grinned.

"He needs his father."

Mitchell gestured around the prisoner's side of the visiting room. "I'm no kind of father, Erin. I know you—you'll find yourself a nice guy, a guy who'd be better for Jason than I ever was."

Why was Kent the man that came to her mind?

"You make it sound like you're giving him up," she said.

Mitchell pushed a hand through his dark hair. "Tammy already signed off her parental rights." His girlfriend had met someone else, who hadn't wanted to raise a prisoner's son, so she'd given Jason to Erin.

"*You* can't," she said. The boy couldn't lose his father as he had his mother.

Mitchell shrugged. "I should. I'm no good for him. You need to meet a nice guy, Erin. A guy who'll take care of both of you."

"I don't need someone to take care of me," she insisted. "And I didn't come here to discuss my love life."

"So you do have one?" he asked with a grin. Despite the glass wall separating them, he was still the big brother teasing his kid sister.

"When would I have time?" she retorted, borrowing Kent's method of answering questions with more questions. "With work and Jason."

"I'm sorry, kid. I've asked too much of you, to take care of my son." He sighed. "If only Randall wasn't such a hard-ass…"

Mitchell had never called her dad, his stepfather, by anything but his first name, even though Mitch had been young when their mom had married Randall Powell.

"I want Jason to live with me," Erin insisted. "I love him so much, Mitchell." As much as she loved her brother.

"So if you didn't come here to discuss your love life, why did you come visit?"

She had yet to ask Kent the free question he'd offered her, because she wasn't sure he'd tell her the truth. She'd come here because she needed Mitchell to reassure her, but she hesitated for the same reason she hesitated asking Kent.

"I—I just wanted to see you," she said.

He grinned again. "I don't know what I'd do without you, Erin. Probably lose my mind. I'm glad you came by."

Now she couldn't ask—because to do so implied that she was beginning to doubt him. Which she was because of Kent. Because she wanted to be able to justify her attraction to him.

But there was no justification. Her brother wouldn't lie to her, so Kent *had* to be.

ANGER PULSED through Kent's veins and pounded at his temples. He'd thought Erin was beginning to change her mind about him and hate him a little less.

He'd been wrong. He clenched the paper in his fist and stabbed at her doorbell with his other hand. "Erin! I know you're working from home." He had already gone by the *Chronicle* looking for her. "Answer the damn door!"

He wasn't worried about his shouting scaring Jason—the boy was at school. He would have Erin all to himself, with no interruptions, to tell her what he *really* thought of her.

The door opened just a few inches, a chain holding it ajar. Dark eyes peered through the crack. "Who are you?"

Like Jason, this person was obviously a relative of Erin's, with the same brown hair, eyes and delicate features.

"I'm Sergeant—"

"Kent Terlecki," the woman finished for him. Then the door closed.

Frustration gnawed at Kent. He fisted his hand to keep from reaching for the doorbell again. And he barely resisted the urge to knock. Obviously Erin wasn't going to even come to the door.

Uttering a ragged sigh, he turned to leave, but then the door opened fully. And the woman who looked so much like Erin, only older, stepped back.

"Come inside, Sergeant," she invited. "Just, please, keep your voice down so you don't wake Jason."

He winced with regret, aware that his yelling upset the little boy. "He's not at school?"

"He's sick."

"So Erin is here," he said. He'd witnessed "Aunt E.'s" protectiveness and couldn't imagine that she would leave the child when he was ill.

"No, she's not, but she doesn't know he's sick. The school couldn't get ahold of her, so they called me. I'm Kathryn Powell. Erin's mother."

He acknowledged the introduction with a brief nod before concern drew him toward the hall leading to the boy's room. "Did he have an asthma attack?" he asked. He glanced back at the woman for an answer and found her staring at him in shock.

"You know about his asthma?"

"Yes." But there was so much else he didn't know. Should he ask this woman why Erin hated him? First, there was something else he needed to know, though. "Is Jason all right?"

She nodded again. "Yes, he did have an asthma attack. The substitute teacher was wearing a lot of perfume."

Kent grimaced in sympathy, as some colognes and perfumes affected his breathing, too. He slipped down the hall and stood in the doorway to the boy's room. Jason was curled into a protective ball beneath his bright-patterned fleece blanket.

"Poor kid," he murmured, resisting the urge to push the sweat-damp brown hair back from the boy's forehead. But he didn't want to disturb him. Reluctantly, he left the child sleeping and returned to where the boy's grandmother stood in the living room. "Is he feeling better?"

"His breathing is back to normal," she assured him, "but he's exhausted. Erin says these attacks always wear him out."

Remembering his own battles, Kent sighed in commiseration. "Yes..."

"You didn't come by to ask about Jason, though," she surmised, glancing down at the copy of the *Chronicle* he clenched in his hand.

His fingers tightened around the paper. "Do you know where Erin is?" he asked.

She sighed in turn. "There's only one place she goes where she can't have her phone with her."

His instincts from years of interviewing witnesses and suspects kicked in, and he sensed she wanted to tell him. So he waited instead of pushing.

"She went to the prison," Kathryn Powell revealed, "to see her brother."

"Jason's father?"

She nodded.

"His last name isn't Powell." He'd checked, after Jason's question at the assembly.

"Mitchell's from my first marriage," she said, staring over Kent's shoulder instead of meeting his gaze, as if she was embarrassed. "His last name is Sullivan."

"Mitchell Sullivan..."

"You probably don't remember him," she said, "but you arrested him four years ago."

Chapter Nine

Erin's temples throbbed. She could have blamed the ache on the siren that had been going off all evening, the sick-sounding wail echoing off the cement walls of the parking structure. But she knew what had brought on her headache—Kent wasn't at class.

"Your turn, Ms. Powell," Lieutenant Michalski said, holding open the driver's door of the idling patrol car. "You're going to be pulling over Ms. Standish."

The mayor's daughter headed toward the unmarked car, a plain black sedan, parked in front of the patrol car. Her high heels clicked against the cement, and the mammoth handbag she carried swung at her side, nearly knocking the petite woman off balance.

Shivering in the gust of wind whipping through the parking garage, Erin ducked into the car. Grateful for the heat blowing out of the vents, she ignored the shotgun mounted barrel up between the seats, and the open laptop, the screen facing her.

Lieutenant Michalski slid into the passenger's seat and directed her attention to the control panel, which operated the lights and sirens. Wincing, she pushed the buttons and proceeded to "pull over" the "speeding" vehicle in front of her.

They'd hardly driven more than a few feet along the parking level. Each member of the CPA had had a turn tonight, playing either the police officer or the speeder so they'd have a little experience and comprehension of procedure before their ride-alongs. The rest of the class huddled together in the parking garage, trying to fight the cold night air. Fortunately, the first part of this evening's session had taken place in the warm conference room.

"You're really lucky, Ms. Powell," the lieutenant commented.

"Lucky that I haven't been tossed out of the program?" she asked. Her reception tonight had been chillier than usual, and it had nothing to do with the weather.

His mouth lifted in a slight grin. "Well, that, too. But I was referring to Ms. Standish. You're the only person who could pull her over without getting reamed out."

"You're saying the chief would yell at you if you gave her a speeding ticket?" she asked.

He laughed. "Not the chief. Her father would be the one yelling."

"Mayor Standish…" Who Kent claimed had a controlling interest in the paper. "So why do you think she joined the Citizen's Police Academy?"

His grin widened. "Same reason you have, Ms. Powell. To spy for the mayor."

"I don't work for the mayor," she protested.

He just shook his head, still smiling, and opened the door. "Okay, everyone, Ms. Powell and Ms. Standish were our last participants, so this traffic stop concludes tonight's class. Please remember," he said, glancing at

Tessa Howard, who wore a skirt that wasn't much shorter than Joelly Standish's, "to dress more appropriately for our outdoor classes."

Even in her sweater, lightweight jacket and jeans, Erin was chilled, so she didn't take offense when everyone disbursed for their vehicles without waiting for her. But Ms. Standish, with her high heels and unwieldy bag, was easy to catch as she headed down the ramp, instead of the stairs, to the lower levels.

"Where are you parked?" Erin asked her.

The woman, who was probably in her early twenties like Erin, shook her head, tossing waves of honey-blond hair around her shoulders. "I didn't drive here."

Did she have a car coming to pick her up? After all, she was Lakewood royalty, and according to some, a spoiled heiress. Her father probably had a chauffeur waiting at her beck and call.

"Do you need a ride somewhere?" Erin asked. "I'd be happy to give you a lift."

Joelly smiled. "Thanks, but where I'm going is close by. I can walk."

Heels on cobblestone sidewalks? Erin doubted it, but obviously this woman, who was nearly as much a class pariah as she was, didn't want her company, either.

Curious to learn more about the mayor's daughter's motives for joining the CPA, Erin persisted. "I was told that this neighborhood can get quite dangerous at night. You really shouldn't walk alone."

"I'm not alone," Joelly said, swinging her mammoth, herringbone-patterned purse out from her narrow shoulder.

A sound emanated from the bag. And when Joelly undid a small flap, a tiny black head popped out. The little dog wriggled, and two ears—each bigger than the face of the bug-eyed critter—popped out, too. Its tiny white teeth bared, the dog growled even as it trembled.

"Shh, Sassy," the woman gently admonished her pet. "Behave."

"What is it?" Erin asked.

"A pit bull trapped in the body of a long-haired Chihuahua." With two fingers Joelly stroked the little head between the ears. "So I'm perfectly safe."

Although the dog considered itself a pit bull, Erin doubted it would fool would-be muggers into thinking the same. But not wanting to antagonize the mayor's daughter, she just smiled. "If you say so…"

The blond woman glanced up from her dog and focused on Erin. Gossip had labeled Joelly Standish a shallow ditz, but her eyes, an odd caramel color, narrowed with surprisingly shrewd intelligence. "I'm not so sure about you, though."

"What do you mean?" Erin swallowed hard, unnerved by the other woman's scrutiny. "Are you talking about how no one likes me?"

"That's your fault. Your column antagonizes them," Joelly pointed out. "I don't think you're in danger, though, because *you're* the one who poses the threat."

"I'm not going to do a story on you," Erin assured her.

Joelly emitted a tinkling laugh that had the dog's ears lifting. "You couldn't if you tried, not at the *Lakewood Chronicle.*"

"I don't understand." In truth, she was actually afraid that she did. She was afraid that Kent Terlecki hadn't lied to her. About anything.

"I used to get a lot of bad press," the heiress admitted.

"So much that my father bought the *Lakewood Chronicle* and promoted his best friend to editor-in-chief." She cocked her head, unconsciously imitating her little dog as it stared at Erin. "Of course, he really didn't do that for me. Or maybe not even to spare himself more embarrassment over me. He probably did it so he could go after the Lakewood Police Department."

Damn Kent Terlecki.

"Why would he do that?"

Joelly smiled. "My father doesn't like to lose."

"What has he lost?" Erin wondered.

"An old girlfriend to Chief Archer. The chief's late wife used to go out with my dad until she met Frank Archer twenty-six years ago."

"That's a long time to hold a grudge," Erin mused, surprised also by how matter-of-factly Joelly spoke about her father's obsession with a woman other than her mother. Somehow she suspected the heiress hadn't had the idyllic upbringing everyone thought she'd had.

Joelly's narrow shoulders lifted in a shrug. "You don't know my dad. I think only his respect for Mrs. Archer kept him in line all these years. But since she died a year ago, he's taken the gloves off and is really going after the chief."

"Why doesn't he just fire him?" Erin asked. "Your father's the mayor."

"But the public loves Chief Archer," Joelly said. "My father…not so much lately."

"And an election's coming up," Erin remembered. "So the mayor has to discredit Chief Archer in the press before he can fire him."

"Or cut the chief's budget, make his life generally miserable and force him to quit," Joelly explained. "But you must know all of this already, or you wouldn't be writing that hateful column of yours."

"I write about Sergeant Terlecki," Erin pointed out, starting to feel ill as she realized her vendetta, not her talent, was why she'd been given her own column.

"Exactly. My father's known Frank Archer a long time. He knows that to get to the chief, he has to go after the people Frank Archer loves the most."

"He loves Kent Terlecki?"

"Yeah, wouldn't you..." Her eyes brightened with amusement. "Oh, you don't know."

"Know what?"

Joelly shook her head. "Despite what people might think, I'm not my father's pawn. And I won't be yours, either, Ms. Powell."

Her little dog swinging in the bag at her side, she headed on down the ramp. But she turned back and advised, "You're the one who needs to be careful."

KENT TIGHTENED HIS GRASP on the dart. He narrowed his eyes, staring toward the board and Erin Powell's beautiful albeit hole-filled face.

"Throw it!" the chief ordered, his voice thick with anger and exasperation.

God, he was losing his edge. How else could people keep sneaking up on him? He turned to his boss. "What are you doing here?" And out of uniform no less, in jeans and a white fisherman's knit sweater.

Frank shrugged shoulders nearly as wide as the entrance to the game area. Even out of uniform, the man was formidable. "I have to eat."

Since his wife had died the year before, he had no

one to cook for him, but what Kent figured bothered Frank most was that he had no one to eat with. Some people couldn't be alone; Kent actually preferred it. Before the shooting, he'd been too busy with work to notice. And now, he couldn't expect someone to put up with the burden he might someday become.

"So what are you going to do about this most recent column?" the chief asked as he propped a shoulder against the archway to the restaurant. He clutched a copy of the *Chronicle* in one hand—the picture that was facing out the same one that stared at Kent from the dartboard. "She called you a 'player.'"

Actually, Billy had called him the *playa.*

Frank Archer snorted. "That proves she doesn't know you at all."

Kent shrugged. "I'm no saint." Although sometimes the chief and his fellow officers tried to treat him like one, which annoyed him no end, since he'd just been doing his job. "I used to date a lot."

"Before the shooting."

"I've dated since the shooting," he insisted.

"Not as much as you did before."

"That's *your* fault," Kent said, then laughed when the chief tensed, probably feeling guilty again. "That *cushy desk job* you gave me takes up more of my time than even the long shifts in vice."

Frank sighed. "I guess you do have to be available pretty much twenty-four–seven."

"So do you." Kent wondered again why his boss had shown up at the Lighthouse. Usually the guy was at his desk, talking with his district captains or meeting with city council members or community leaders.

"My wife understood." As ever, the chief's bright blue eyes dimmed when he mentioned his late wife. "I don't guess your girlfriends have."

"Nope."

"But no one *mis*understands you like Ms. Powell does." Archer lifted the paper to eye level and, squinting in the dim light of the game area, read from Erin's column. "'Sergeant Kent Terlecki uses his questionable charm to garner good press for himself and the department. He's clearly willing to take his oath to a whole new level—to protect and *service.*'"

A laugh rumbled out of Kent's chest even though just the day before he had been furious over the column she'd written, Public Information Officer Pimped for PR.

"You think it's funny?"

"I didn't," he admitted. "But now I can see the humor in it."

"She's trying to make you and the department look foolish." Archer bristled. He wasn't old enough to be Kent's dad, but that didn't stop him from acting like he was. "How's your investigation into her background going? Have you found a motive for her persecution of you?"

Kent sighed. "Yeah…yeah, I have…."

"So? What is it?"

"I arrested her brother four years ago." He had pulled the report and the transcripts from the trial. That was why he'd had to get out of the office. He'd had to get away from the irrefutable evidence that he and Erin had no future. He'd already known it, of course, but now he couldn't even try to fool himself that if not for the bullet, they might have had something.

Archer groaned. "What did you arrest him for?"

"Dealing."

"How long did he get?"

"Ten years." Ten years out of his son's life. When Mitchell got released, Jason would be almost a teenager.

Frank whistled. "He had a lot of drugs in his possession then."

"Yeah." Reading his report had brought back the details for Kent. "He was dealing out of an off campus apartment that he shared with his girlfriend and two year old son." Kent's heart clenched when he remembered Jason, as a toddler, screaming when the special response team broke down the door.

"That much product, he had to be midlevel," Frank mused.

"Yeah, one of the dealers under him—a college kid—gave him up to me."

"Erin's brother didn't give you any names of people higher up, to reduce his sentence?"

"Nope."

"Too loyal or too scared?"

"Too stubborn." Like his sister.

"So this is why she's after you and the department? Because her brother got caught?"

He remembered what her mother had shared. "She thinks I framed him—that I did it to pad my arrest record and get the promotion to my cushy desk job."

Archer laughed. "Doesn't she realize how much was seized? You couldn't have planted that much evidence."

"I wouldn't have planted *any* evidence *ever.*"

"I know that. Everyone who knows you knows that."

The chief crumpled the paper. "Ms. Powell clearly doesn't know you."

Kent sighed. He'd thought she was getting to know him—when she'd kissed him like she had in her kitchen.

"You need to tell her about yourself," the chief advised. "*Everything* about yourself."

Kent had no intention of telling her about the bullet, but he asked, "You really think that's going to make a difference?"

Frank shook his head. "Probably not."

Kent walked toward the dartboard. "It's easier for her to blame me." Realizing now her animosity really wasn't personal, he corrected, "It's easier for a person to blame the arresting officer than to admit their relative has done something wrong—something criminal."

"You're not likely to forget that," the chief commented. "You have a bullet in your spine to remind you of that."

And just as the bullet would always be with Kent, the animosity and resentment toward the officer who had arrested her brother would always be with Erin. She would never forgive him. So their uncertain future was not uncertain at all. They had *no* future.

He pulled out the dart at the top of the board, the one that had pinned her picture to it, and he took down the tattered portrait of Erin Powell. He didn't want to hurt her anymore.

HAND TREMBLING FROM the cold, Erin struggled to fit the key in the lock. The door suddenly opened before she could unlock it.

"You're freezing," her mother observed.

"Most of the class took place outside tonight," Erin

said as she hurried into the warmth of the living room, which her mother had, as always, tidied. Erin lifted the folded fleece throw from the back of the couch and wrapped it around her shoulders.

"You're home early," Kathryn noted, with some surprise.

"Dad wasn't happy the past couple of weeks that you drove back home so late." Erin doubted her father was going to be happy no matter what time her mother came home, because he didn't like his wife watching Mitchell's son. Instead of rejoicing in the birth of their grandson, they'd been embarrassed that the child had been born out of wedlock.

"So you came home early because you didn't want to upset your father?" Mom asked, her voice sharp with skepticism.

Erin shook her head. "I just came home early…."

Because Kent hadn't been part of the traffic-stop class. He hadn't even put in an appearance.

"If you wanted to make your father happy, you'd quit writing that column of yours," her mother advised, with her usual disapproval.

"That column is paying to keep a roof over Jason's and my head."

"We're not saying to stop writing for the *Chronicle,* just change the tone of your articles, Erin," Kathryn Powell requested. "You wouldn't lose your job if you did that."

Erin wasn't so sure about that—not after talking to Joelly Standish in the parking garage. Kent had been right. The mayor owned the paper and was using it for his personal vendetta.

She pulled the blanket tighter around her shoulders,

but couldn't dispel the chill. "I don't want to alter the tone of my articles, Mom."

"I thought you might be changing your mind about Kent Terlecki."

"Why would you think that?" she asked. "Haven't you been reading my column?"

"Your father and I wish you'd accept the truth, Erin," Kathryn said, her voice more gentle than disapproving. "We wish you'd stop wasting your time going after the police department. I know that's the only reason you're taking this class—"

And maybe that was why her father didn't approve of her mother watching Jason.

"Trying to prove my brother's innocence is not a waste of my time," Erin insisted.

"You can't prove what isn't true," her mom said quietly, and she reached out and brushed her hand tenderly along Erin's cheek. "You have to accept that Mitchell isn't that older brother you idolized when you were young. Even before he left home, he was getting into trouble. He had fallen in with the wrong crowd."

"He made some mistakes," Erin admitted. "He was smoking and drinking, but that's a long way from dealing drugs, Mom. He wouldn't do that."

"You don't want to believe that he would," her mother said with a soft sigh. "But he isn't that boy you used to know, Erin."

"He says he didn't do it, Mom." That should have been good enough for her, but now those doubts had niggled—because of Kent.

Her mother shook her head, as if resigned. "He needs to take responsibility for his mistakes."

"Mom..."

Kathryn lifted her chin and forced her lips into a tight smile. "Let's not talk about Mitchell then."

"Good, because we're never going to agree." She couldn't turn her back on her brother the way her parents had. She couldn't betray him with the officer responsible for putting him behind bars.

"Let's talk about Sergeant Terlecki," her mother suggested.

Heat flooded Erin's body, warming her more than the blanket, as she thought about her and Kent in the kitchen. If not for Jason interrupting them, they might have made love right on the edge of the sink. She swallowed back the desire, the guilt choking her. "What about Kent Terlecki?"

"Is it him—is he this *Sarge*—that Jason's been talking nonstop about?"

Erin nodded, glad that she hadn't corrected Jason. She preferred that he didn't refer to Kent by his real name; it was less personal.

"So it seems that Jason has gotten over his fear of police officers," her mother said with a genuine smile of relief. "That little boy is in awe of Sergeant Terlecki."

"He's too young to know better," Erin pointed out. "Too young to resist Kent's charm." So what was her excuse? How come, whenever he came near her, she couldn't resist him, either? It was good that she hadn't seen him for a while; maybe she could remember what was important to her. Her brother. Her nephew. Her family.

Not Kent Terlecki. He meant nothing to her.

Chapter Ten

Erin's fingers hesitated over the keyboard. She wanted to write about last night's class of the CPA, about the explanation of the pursuit policy, when an officer made a decision whether or not to pursue a speeding vehicle based on the risk. But she knew Herb Stein wouldn't print that column. He wanted another article about Kent or the department, something negative to further the mayor's agenda.

If she'd still been that idealistic girl she'd once been, she would have quit on principle alone, but she needed a job, needed to keep her apartment. Sure, she could probably move back to her parents' place. Her father might even get over his disapproval of Mitchell and accept his step-grandson.

But if she left Lakewood, she wouldn't be able to prove her brother's innocence. At the same time, she wasn't certain how to do that even if she stayed. For the past year she had investigated Kent Terlecki and had found out very little about him besides what she'd read in police reports. His fellow officers and friends would answer no questions about him. She didn't even know why they called him Bullet, so how was she going to find out if he had framed her brother? Overwhelmed with frustration, she pounded her fists on the keys.

"Writing not going well?" A blond head popped over the top of the fabric divider that separated Erin's desk from those of the other reporters in the "pit."

Relieved to get her mind off Kent and her job, Erin smiled at Tessa Howard. "So did you get it?"

"The *Chronicle* account?" Tessa patted her ever-present black briefcase. "Of course I did. We're going to handle all your telecommunication needs from now on. Thanks for the reference."

"I'm sure you got the account all on your own," Erin assured her. "My reference wouldn't mean a whole lot around here."

"You're the star reporter—at least one article in every issue and now a columnist, no less," Tessa said. "I'm sure your opinion carries weight around here."

On the contrary, Erin thought. She was carrying more guilt that she wasn't doing more, that she couldn't help Reverend Thomas or talk about the real purpose of the Citizen's Police Academy.

"No." She lowered her voice and replied, "Not many of my coworkers are happy that I have my own column after working here just a year."

Tessa shrugged. "Don't let it bother you. Sure, I'd like my coworkers to be friends, too, but they're really just competitors."

"I can understand that in a sales job, but..." She swallowed a sigh of self-pity. She had never indulged in that, not when she was fully aware of how many people were in worse situations than hers.

"Make friends somewhere else," Tessa suggested. "Like class."

Erin laughed. "You're one of the few people in the CPA who doesn't hate my column."

"*Few?*" Tessa asked, skeptically arching a blond brow as she grinned.

"*Only.*"

"Is that why you didn't come by the bar after last night's class?" Tessa settled onto a corner of Erin's tiny metal desk.

She shrugged. "I needed to get home to my nephew. My mom doesn't like driving back to East Grand Rapids so late at night."

"I have some accounts in Grand Rapids. It's a long drive," Tessa agreed. "If you ever need someone to watch Jason, you can bring him by my house. My mom's taking Wednesday nights off, so she can watch the kids."

Tessa didn't have children of her own, but she had taken on much of the responsibility for her younger siblings to help out her single mom.

"Thanks for the offer," Erin said, "but Jason's…" Her heart swelled with affection. "He's a really sweet, *shy* boy."

"He would have to know someone awhile before he'd be comfortable staying with them," Tessa surmised, with her usual quick understanding. "That has to be tough on you, though, with your folks living over an hour away. My mom's pretty much always been on her own, but she had her mom until Nana died."

"And now she has you," Erin said, wondering how much of her life Tessa had sacrificed to help out with her family. She was right. You didn't have to look much further to find someone who'd made more sacrifices or who was in a tougher situation than you were. She smiled. "I'm sure no one missed me at the Lighthouse, anyway."

"*I* missed you."

Warmth lifted Erin's flagging spirits. "Thank you."

"I mean it." Tessa grabbed her hand and squeezed. "But, hey, I know you're busy here—" she gestured toward the keyboard "—pounding out your next column. I also understand that you're busy at home with Jason, but if you ever need a friend..."

Since moving to Lakewood, Erin hadn't had time to make friends or to renew her relationships with the ones she'd left behind in East Grand Rapids when she'd gone off to college, then the Peace Corps.

"I could use one," she freely admitted. "I just can't believe you would want to be my friend."

"The best part of the CPA has been getting to know people," Tessa said.

Erin wondered if she was including Lieutenant Chad Michalski in her statement. At the last class, she had seemed less resentful of what she'd considered his manipulating her to the join the academy.

"I know there's more to you than this column," Tessa continued. "You're obviously devoted to your nephew. You're a good person."

"Thank you." She'd needed that endorsement, because she didn't feel like a good person anymore. She had changed into this bitter, vengeful one even she didn't like.

"You're a little misguided maybe," Tessa said with a teasing chuckle, "but still a good person. Do you want to grab some lunch?"

"I'd love to," Erin said, yearning for the companionship, not the food. "But I need to finish this."

"Another time then," Tessa promised as she slid off Erin's desk and left. She had only been gone a moment before Herb Stein poked his head around the partition.

Erin swallowed hard, aware that the editor-in-chief rarely visited the "pit." He usually had reporters summoned to *his* office. She didn't know whether to be flattered or afraid.

"How's the column coming?" he asked.

"Fine," she lied.

"So what's your focus this week?"

"Sergeant Terlecki wasn't at last night's class," she warned him. "Lieutenant Michalski, the department's emergency vehicle operation expert, explained the pursuit policy and had us participate in simulated traffic stops."

Herb exaggerated a yawn. "You're not writing about that. You must have seen Terlecki since last week's class."

At her dinner table. In her kitchen. Up close and way too personal. "He spoke at an assembly at my nephew's school."

Herb nodded. "There has to be some angle you can work there."

The truth. That Kent had been wonderful with those kids. But she suspected telling him that would put her boss to sleep.

"Hell, every time I turn on the news I see Terlecki's face." The older man swiped a hand down over his own face, his jowls jiggling against his neck, then focused on Erin. "He sure is a handsome devil."

Hell, yes. She masked her real feelings with a shrug and an outright lie. "I hadn't noticed."

"Plenty of women have." Herb grimaced. "Even my own wife. And like you pointed out in your last column, he uses his *charm* to get good press from the networks."

She suspected now that was only because the mayor didn't own them.

"That was a strategic move on the chief's part to put Terlecki in charge of the media," Herb said. "But I'm glad the *Chronicle* has one reporter who can't be fooled."

She wasn't certain she could still claim that distinction. "I'd really like to write more about the class," she persisted. "I think the public would be interested in why an officer sometimes chooses not to pursue a fleeing vehicle." Often the risk to the community was too great and because a high-speed chase could endanger pedestrians or other drivers.

"I haven't been wrong about you, have I?" he asked, a threat apparent in his sharp tone.

She thought of Kent's sensitivity with Jason that first night when his raised voice had scared the little boy, and then how diplomatically he'd answered Jason's question at the assembly and how he'd talked to him during dinner.

How could she keep writing horrible things about a man like that? Maybe, just as she wasn't the same idealistic girl who'd served in the Peace Corps, he wasn't the same ambitious young officer who'd possibly framed her brother.

"I knew I was taking a chance hiring you, but then I took an even bigger chance giving you this column..." Herb Stein shook his head and grimaced in disgust. "Maybe there isn't a place for you here."

"No, sir, I won't let you down," she promised.

Her boss studied her through narrowed eyes.

"Terlecki's not getting to you like he has those other reporters who fawn all over him?"

Tightening her jaw, she shook her head. "He hasn't gotten to me at all," she promised. "I'll give you a column you'll like."

But Kent wouldn't. He'd said before he didn't hate her, but she knew it was just a matter of time before he would.

THE WORDS GREW JUMBLED as Kent rubbed his eyes, unable to read any more of Erin's column. She had even turned around the school assembly to make him look bad. He read the last line aloud, "'Trying to make impressionable kids believe he's a hero…'"

"If you really wanted to do that, you'd tell them about the bullet in your back," the chief commented from where he leaned in the doorway of Kent's office. "Better yet, you'd tell *her*."

"I'm not going to do that." Mainly because he didn't trust himself to talk to her at all right now. He was too damn mad. He also didn't want any more people to know about his injury and especially not about Mrs. Ludlow's role in it. The woman had suffered enough.

"So you still think it's better that she doesn't learn the truth about you?" Frank Archer asked.

Kent shrugged. "If learning the truth about me means learning the truth about her brother, I'm not sure I can do that to her." Even as pissed off as he was…"Then there's her brother's kid to consider…."

"Ms. Powell is not a little kid," the chief pointed out. "*She* should know the truth. And after writing this trash—" the chief waved the paper disdainfully "—she doesn't deserve any consideration from you."

Kent winced as he rose from his chair to pace the small floor space around his desk. "Her mom is the one who told me about her brother being in prison." He'd promised Kathryn Powell that he wouldn't tell Erin where he'd learned that information.

"Her brother is in prison because of *you,*" Archer said. "I mean, because of your arrest."

"Erin sees it the other way," Kent corrected. "That it's my fault—and only my fault—that her brother's in prison."

"It's *his* fault," Frank said. "He's the one who broke the law."

"She can't bring herself to admit it." Kent remembered what else her mother had shared with him—all of her and her husband's regrets that they had paid more attention to his students than their own children, and that they had worried more about what the school and the church community thought than about their kids. "She idolizes her brother."

"Like the rookies idolize you."

Kent shook his head. "She's worshipped her brother her whole life. Her dad and mom were always busy with school stuff. Her dad's a teacher, so Mitchell spent the most time with Erin while they were growing up, and he doted on her."

"Spoiled her," Frank commented.

"Loved her." Kent sighed. "And she loves him. He has her completely convinced that he's innocent and that I framed him."

Frank ran a hand around the back of his neck. "So no matter how much proof you give her, she's never going to believe you over her brother."

"He's her hero."

"But you're the real hero." The chief patted Kent's shoulder. "And if she learns that, she might realize that her brother is not the man she thinks he is."

"Right." That was another reason Kent was reluctant to tell her. He didn't want to hurt her any more than her brother being in jail already had.

"That's not your problem." The chief waved the paper once more. "*This* is."

"I know." Kent winced again, but the pain wasn't in his back. "I know it's *my* job to handle the media. So I will understand if you decide to replace me with someone else."

Frank straightened away from the jamb, his long body tense with shock. "Why the hell would I do that?"

"She's not going to stop writing about me until her brother either admits the truth or is released from prison."

"That's why you need to tell her—"

"We already agreed she's not going to believe what *I* tell her," Kent reminded his boss. "And hell, if I try to convince her that her brother's lying…"

"She'll lash out more. What if you showed her the files?"

"She's already seen everything." Kent was positive.

"Her brother has her brainwashed," the chief said with a snort of disgust.

"She's loyal." It was one of the things Kent admired about her, even though it also infuriated him. Not only was she loyal, she was loving. If not for her brother's arrest, she still would have been that idealistic girl who'd entered the Peace Corps out of college.

"The department can't afford the bad press right

now," Kent said. "The only way she's going to lay off me—and the department—is if you let me go."

"That's not going to happen, son," the chief said, placing his hand on Kent's shoulder.

"But you have to think about what's best for the department," Kent insisted.

"I have to think about what's best for *you*. You should give an interview to one of the networks. Maybe that red-haired reporter," Archer suggested. "Tell her, on camera, what's really going on at the *Lakewood Chronicle*. That *Powell on Patrol* has a vendetta against you for arresting her drug-dealing brother."

Maybe the chief should have been doing Kent's job all along. "I can't do that…."

"Why are you so worried about Erin Powell?" Frank asked. "Do you have feelings for her?"

"That would be crazy," Kent said.

Archer nodded. "Yeah, it would. As crazy as me letting you go."

"I'd rather leave than…" Hurt Erin or Jason. They'd both been through enough already.

"Then do that interview." The chief furrowed his brow, studying him. "You must really care about her."

Catching the disbelief on his boss's face, Kent nearly laughed. Frank clearly thought his public information officer had lost his mind. *God, maybe he had.* Why couldn't he stop thinking about her, about that day in her kitchen and her kisses?

"Her brother's son lives with her," Kent shared. "Here in Lakewood, where that interview you suggested would air."

Archer nodded with sudden understanding. "So she

wouldn't be the only one to get hurt if her true motives came out. The boy would suffer, too, with everyone knowing the truth about his dad."

"Kids can be cruel. And with his small size and health problems, Jason's already an underdog."

"Jason?" The chief whistled. "Wow, you might not have been in the field the past three years, but you still remember how to do a thorough investigation."

"I've met him. He's a neat kid." Kent's heart warmed just thinking of the brave little boy asking the question he had. "He's already lost so much."

"I can't afford to lose *you*," Frank said, his voice raspy with emotion as he probably remembered the time he nearly had lost Kent. "You're not going anywhere. So you better figure some other way to handle Ms. Powell."

He'd like to handle her again—to hold her in his arms and finish what they had started that night in her kitchen. But glancing down at the paper the chief dropped on his desk, Kent realized the best way to deal with Erin Powell was to stay far away from her.

Chapter Eleven

Erin shivered as she stepped outside, though it was actually warmer in the cool night air than it had been inside the Lighthouse. Except for Tessa, everyone hated her, but not nearly as much as Erin was beginning to hate herself.

She didn't know how much longer she could keep up the "tone" her boss wanted for the column. After how sweet Kent had been with Jason, she had to struggle to hang on to her anger and resentment.

But confusion clouded her judgment and her vision. Was she betraying Mitchell with the doubts Kent had stirred up in her along with her attraction to him? Or was she betraying herself by continuing to write a column so far removed from the reporter she had wanted to be back in college and the Peace Corps? The one who would rather have written about Reverend Thomas's shelter for runaways, or Rafe Sanchez's after-school youth center, than Kent's visit to Maple Valley Elementary.

Guilt tugged at her. He'd been so sensitive when he'd answered Jason's question, but she hadn't included that detail in her latest column. Instead, she'd been snarky and had deliberately misconstrued his intentions. She blinked back the threat of tears and reached out toward her van with the remote keyless entry switch, opening the locks.

No one had walked out with her; no one had offered. The only comments she'd gotten at all tonight had been that she'd stepped over the line. But now she heard something like the scrape of shoes against cement, and she reached inside her purse for her canister of pepper spray. She whirled around, but could see no one in the deep shadows.

"You want the truth about Bullet?"

"Who's there?" she called out, her voice cracking with nerves. She'd received plenty of complaints by e-mail, letter and voice mail about her columns. Was someone actually going to confront her physically now? Her grip tightened around the pepper spray.

The man, tall and wiry with dark hair and a beard, stepped into the light. "Do you want to know how he came by his nickname?"

"You're vice, right, Sergeant Halliday?" she asked, recognizing the man from the first class of the CPA and from the night she'd eavesdropped on his and Kent's conversation at the bar. "You're a friend of Sergeant Terlecki's."

"Yes," Billy said with pride, "but Kent is friends with everyone who really knows him."

"And you really know him?"

"We share a house," he explained, "when I'm not undercover."

"So if you're such good friends, why would you talk to me?" she wondered. "Why would you tell me anything, especially something that Kent has been working pretty hard to keep from me?"

Billy shook his head. "He isn't keeping anything from you. You are just too determined to see anything but the truth where Kent is concerned. And that's too bad."

"Why?"

"Because I think, despite what a bitch you've been to him, that he likes you." He shook his head as if disgusted. "Something about you attracts him."

"I have a pulse."

"Kent's not a player. I was razzing him that night you overheard us talking at the bar. Sure, Channel 7 would like to be involved with him, but he's not interested in her." Billy snorted and added, "He's interested in *you.*"

Erin's pulse leaped. "He…he—"

"You can't deny it," Billy interrupted. "You know he is."

His kisses had told her as much, but still she argued, "He's just trying to charm me the way he has *Channel 7* so that I'll write more favorably about him and the department."

Billy snorted again. "If that was his intention, it doesn't seem to be working for him."

It was working more than Erin cared to admit. The memory of his touch kept her awake nights, imagining what they could have—if they were different people. If he hadn't been the officer who'd arrested her brother…

"But that's not what he's doing," Billy insisted. "He's not that guy you're trying to make him out to be."

"What guy is he?" she asked almost flippantly, even though she really wanted to know. She *needed* to know.

"He's the *kind* of guy," Billy said, his voice full of emotion, "who takes a *bullet* for another guy."

Erin's heart clenched with the realization of what

his friend was telling her. "He got *shot?* He took a bullet. For you?"

"For the chief. Three years ago. That's where he got his nickname." Billy's dark eyes glistened with emotion and pride in his friend. "Because he still has one in his spine."

"What—" Erin swallowed the tears burning her throat as she reeled from the revelation. In the year she had been living in Lakewood, she hadn't heard about any officer getting shot. *Ever.* She hadn't even briefly considered that as a possible reason for his moniker. "What happened?"

"He jumped into the line of fire," Billy explained. "Shielded the chief with his body, saving Chief Archer's life without a care about his own."

She closed her eyes to shut out the image, but it played through her mind. Kent protecting the chief, the bullet striking his body. His blood seeping out of the wound, staining his black uniform as it spilled from his body. She gasped as if someone had slammed a fist into her stomach.

"How—how bad was it?" she managed to ask, hoping that what she'd just imagined was worse than the reality.

"We almost lost him," Billy said, confirming her fears. "His heart stopped beating a couple of times, but they shocked him back. He lost so much blood...."

She couldn't think about that. Instead she focused on what had happened. "You said he still has a bullet in his spine?"

"They couldn't get it out," his friend said, rubbing a hand over his beard as if struggling with the memories of that dark time, "not without paralyzing him."

"Oh, my God..." Paralyzed. The thought of Kent, so

strong and healthy, being disabled by an act of heroism... She blinked hard, fighting the sting of tears. "But how could they just leave it in? Doesn't it bother him?"

"He won't admit it, not even to me, but I see the pain on his face. It keeps him awake some nights. Other times if he moves too quickly, turns too sharply, a look crosses his face." Billy expelled a ragged sigh. "I know he's hurting like hell."

"He grimaces." She remembered that look when the little girl from Jason's class had climbed into his arms. Erin had physically felt his pain.

"Yeah." Billy nodded. "You noticed then."

She had noticed more than she'd realized about Kent. "I wondered..." She drew in a shaky breath. "But I never imagined..."

"He didn't want you to know." Billy shook his head. "I'm going to catch hell for telling you."

"Was it just *me* he didn't want to know? Because he worried that I might write an article about it?"

Billy uttered a humorless chuckle. "I think we all know there's no way you'll ever write anything flattering about Kent. No. He hates it when *anyone* finds out what happened to him."

"Why?"

The sergeant shrugged. "He doesn't want them thinking he's a hero."

"But he is. He saved the chief's life." She didn't doubt that Billy Halliday had told her the truth. Something about the man, despite his scruffy appearance, inspired her confidence. Like his mother, he was too straightforward to attempt to trick her.

"Kent absolutely hates it when people treat him like

a hero, when they treat him differently." Billy laughed. "Maybe that's why he likes you. You've certainly never done that."

"No, I haven't." The guilt increased, weighing on her. "I wish I'd known...."

"Would it have changed what you've written about him?" Billy asked.

"I don't know," she replied. It certainly added to her confusion now, and her concern for him. "What about his pain? Can't they do anything for him? Can't they try again to get the bullet out?"

The sergeant shrugged. "There wasn't a whole lot they could do for him without putting him in a wheelchair. But leaving the bullet in isn't real safe, either—scar tissue can cause nerve damage. That's why he can't get medical clearance to do his job now. That's why he's been desked."

"Desked?" she asked.

"Taken out of the field." Billy shuddered, as if the thought inspired nightmares. "That probably hurt Kent more than the gunshot wound."

"Hurt him?" She had thought that he'd wanted his cushy desk job. Clearly she'd thought wrong.

"Kent thrived in the field. He had the highest arrest record for a reason. He loved doing his job."

"So he wasn't promoted?" She'd always considered his move his motive for framing her brother. But if that wasn't it, why would he have...?

"The chief sees it that Kent earned his job."

"By taking the bullet meant for him."

"By being the best damn police officer Lakewood's ever had," Billy said defensively.

"You are a good friend."

"I'm not a fool," he said, his dark eyes burning with righteous anger. "I see the man Kent really is."

"And that is?"

"He's a hero. Why don't you print *that?*" he challenged.

"Because I didn't know…."

"That makes you a pretty lousy reporter," he said, "don't you think?"

Erin silently agreed with the vice cop's critical assessment. Because of Mitchell, she had lost her objectivity. But learning about Kent's heroism had only made her lose more—maybe her heart….

KENT LAY ON THE hardwood floor, breathing deeply and slowly, willing himself to relax so that the tense muscles in his back would do the same. He closed his eyes, but then saw her face—the delicate features, the fathomless brown eyes—and he tensed again, grimacing at the spasm of pain that clutched him.

"Dammit…"

The ringing of the telephone punctuated his curse. Maybe he should have forced the chief to accept his resignation. Then he wouldn't have to be available twenty-four–seven anymore. He grabbed the cordless receiver with a terse greeting. "Terlecki here."

"Can you come over?" a female voice asked.

His breath shuddered out with surprise. "Erin?"

"Yes," she said, almost shyly. "Can you come over? I want to talk to you."

Bitterness and resentment welled up in a short laugh. "The problem is not your talking to me, Erin. The problem is when I talk to you, you twist every damn word I say to you." He snorted. "Hell, you twist everything I say to everyone. Even to your nephew…"

"I know," she quietly agreed. "You have no reason to trust me."

"I have no reason to talk to you," he said, even if it was his damn job. For the moment. "So, what? You need another quote for your next column?"

"Kent, please come over," she implored, "or tell me where you live. I'll come to you. We need to talk."

"I have nothing to say to you but goodbye." Hand shaking, Kent clicked off the phone, then flung it across the room, where it struck the wainscoting and bounced onto the floor. "Damn her!"

Hell, maybe he did need to talk to her. She was a big girl—big enough to take on him and the entire police department. She could handle learning the truth about her brother. Maybe it was about time someone told her. Maybe it was about damn time *he* told her.

Sure, she wouldn't believe him, as he'd warned the chief, but at least everything would be out in the open between them. She'd know he was aware that her grudge against him was the reason for her venomous articles.

The pain in his back forgotten—for the moment—he vaulted to his feet, grabbed his jacket and the file on her brother. Then he opened the door, to find Billy about to jab the key in the lock.

"What the heck," Kent said in surprise. "I thought you were deep cover."

"I have to talk to you," his roommate said, but his voice dragged with reluctance.

Concern for his friend tugged at Kent. "Is it life or death?" he asked.

Billy shook his head.

"Then it's going to have to wait. There's someone else I need to talk to right now." Not that he expected her to listen.

ERIN PACED THE FLOOR between her living room and the small foyer, stepping over toys and books. She should have asked Billy where he and Kent lived. She could have gone over to see him, because she doubted he would come to see her, not after hanging up on her.

But she couldn't blame him after the way she'd persecuted him in the press. Shame clutched at her, tightening the muscles in her stomach until she felt physically ill. In her defense, she had only been avenging what she had believed was Kent's injustice against her brother.

She drew to a sudden stop, shocked at her betrayal of her brother. Why should she doubt now what Mitchell had told her? He had never lied to her before. Just because Kent had saved the chief's life didn't mean that he hadn't destroyed her brother's.

Yet what had been his motive, since he hadn't wanted the promotion to his desk job? Kent had no reason to frame her brother.

Had she been wrong about everything and everyone?

The bell pealed in the foyer, startling her. She pulled open the door, not entirely surprised that she had been wrong *again*. "I thought you weren't coming…."

Chapter Twelve

"I shouldn't have come," Kent said. Just seeing her beautiful face drained away his anger, leaving only pain. And desire.

"I'm glad you did," she countered, but her brown eyes filled with confusion as if she doubted what she claimed, as if she wished he hadn't. She stepped back and gestured him inside, then closed the door behind him.

Keeping his voice to a whisper, he asked, "Where's Jason? Is he in bed?"

"He's at my mom and dad's," she replied. "Mom got sick of driving home after dark and brought him back with her tonight. He actually fell asleep over there."

Kent picked up on the surprise in her voice. "He's never spent the night before?"

She shook her head. "He usually doesn't like to be apart from me. I have a struggle just to drop him at school every morning."

"Separation anxiety." He closed his eyes, remembering the screaming toddler he'd lifted from his crib four years ago. Kent had taken away Jason's father, his family. The poor kid hadn't had Erin then; she'd been in the

Peace Corps and out of the country. What about the grandparents—had they been there for the little kid when he'd needed them most? "Isn't Jason close to your parents?"

She managed a slight smile. "Randall and Kathryn Powell aren't really comfortable with being grandparents."

Yeah, he'd picked up on that himself. But he and her mother had agreed to keep their conversation that day from Erin, neither seeing the point in bringing it up since it would only upset her. "Jason is six," he remembered. "Haven't they gotten used to him yet?"

"He hasn't been around them that much," she explained. "His mother gave him to me only a year ago."

"She gave him away?"

Erin nodded, her eyes filling with sympathy. "She wasn't exactly mother-of-the-year material. According to Jason, she dumped him on her parents a lot so she could go out to 'grown-up' places. Her parents moved to Florida around the time she got serious about a guy she'd met. He didn't want to raise another man's kid, so she signed off her parental rights to Jason."

"I'd say poor kid, but I think he's actually lucky." As angry as Erin made him, he knew she loved her nephew. "He has you now."

Her eyes glistened with emotion. "I'm the lucky one."

"What about Jason's father?" he asked, wondering if she was ready to tell him about Mitchell. Was that why she'd wanted him to come over?

She shook her head. "I didn't ask you to come over to talk about my family."

Kent was glad now that he'd shoved the file on her

brother into the inside pocket of his jacket. "What did you want to talk about?" he asked.

"You." Her delicate throat moved as she swallowed. "I'm sorry."

"About your column?" He hadn't expected an apology from her.

Color rushed to her face. "I should apologize for that."

"But you're not?"

"You were right, you know," she said with a sad smile, "about my boss and the mayor."

His anger dissipated. "So he's forcing you to keep it negative?"

"Let's just say he's *encouraging* me." She sighed. "What I'm sorry about is not believing that you're a hero. Because you are." She stared up at him, her brown eyes wide with the awe that always annoyed him whenever anyone found out what he'd done for the chief.

He winced, hating that she knew.

"Are you hurting?" she asked, instantly solicitous.

"No," he said, but he wouldn't have admitted it even if he still was.

"You were, that day at the school, when you lifted that little girl after the assembly. I saw you grimace. It hurt you to lift her."

"It was how I twisted, not the lifting," he explained. "I can still lift weights, still work out…."

"But you can't do your job—the job you *really* love."

If she still believed he was responsible for her brother being behind bars, she would have been happy that he couldn't. But she wasn't happy.

"I'm fine." Yet he had some concern that he wasn't—that the bullet was shifting or that scar tissue was building up on his nerves. He would have to take the chief's advice and see another specialist soon.

"You're a hero," she repeated with a breathy sigh.

"Stop saying that. I'm not," he insisted, irritation fraying his patience. "I didn't do anything that anyone else in the department wouldn't have done."

"But they didn't step in front of that bullet," she said. "You did."

"It was reflex," he said dismissively. "Nothing more."

"Why won't you take credit for it?" she asked. "Why didn't you tell me about it?"

He raised his brows. "Would you have believed me?"

"Probably not," she admitted. "I would have figured you'd made it up to impress me, to get me to change my mind about you."

"So why do you believe it now?" he asked.

"You didn't tell me."

"Who gave me up?" Then he nodded, understanding his housemate's sudden necessity to talk. "Billy."

She smiled. "Don't be mad at him. He's a good friend to you."

Kent sighed. "Yeah. So you trust Billy but not me?"

"I might have believed you if you told me now," she said.

"So you're beginning to trust me? Enough to ask your free question and trust that I'll give you a truthful answer?"

She hesitated just long enough to reveal her feelings.

"You're never going to trust me." It wouldn't matter if he showed her the file. She would never believe him over her brother. He turned for the door.

She caught his arm, holding him back. "I'm trying, Kent. I *want* to believe you."

To believe him, though, she would have to doubt her brother, and she was too loyal for that. He expelled a ragged sigh of frustration.

"This is impossible," he said, turning back to her. "Despite all this, I can't stop wanting you."

"I want you, too."

Dread curled in his stomach. He'd had the groupies like that college girl in the CPA, who had pursued him once they'd found out about the shooting. "Would you want me if you didn't know about the bullet?"

She laughed. "I kissed you—*twice*—before I found out about it."

"So kiss me again," he urged her.

ERIN SHIVERED in anticipation as she lifted one hand to the nape of Kent's neck. Her fingers delved into his soft blond hair, pulling his head down to hers. She rose on tiptoe and slanted her mouth across his.

His arms circled her, dragging her close against him. Her breasts molded to the hard muscles of his chest. Yet they weren't close enough—too many layers of clothing separated them.

She opened her mouth to deepen their kiss, to invite him inside. His tongue stroked across her bottom lip, in and out. Passion built inside her, burning low in her stomach. "Kent..."

He eased away, his hands sliding up her back to her shoulders, then he gently cupped her face in his palms. "Erin, are you sure?"

Need overwhelmed her, trivializing her doubts, and she nodded. She covered his hands with hers and pulled them away from her face. Entwining their fingers, she tugged him toward the hall. Walking backward, she missed Jason's toy car until the hard plastic bit into the sole of her bare foot. She stumbled, but Kent grabbed her.

She caught the grimace that briefly twisted his handsome face. "Your back!"

"Is fine," he assured her. And as if to prove it, he bent forward and tossed her over his broad shoulder, carrying her down the hall toward her bedroom.

"Put me down," she implored him. "You're going to hurt yourself."

He dropped her onto the mattress. "I am hurting," he admitted. "I'm hurting for you." He lowered himself onto her. The erection that strained the fly of his jeans pushed into the cradle of her hips.

She shifted beneath him, her desire for him becoming almost painful as it built inside her. Hands trembling, she pushed his leather jacket from his shoulders.

He kissed her, his mouth hard and insistent as his lips parted hers and his tongue delved inside. His hands moved beneath the hem of her sweatshirt, lifting it to reveal her bare breasts. He pulled back, his eyes darkening as he stared down at her.

"I didn't think you were coming," she said, embarrassed now that she'd changed into her ratty sweatshirt and a pair of cotton pajama bottoms.

His mouth curved into that sexy grin. "So you didn't dress for me."

She shook her head. "But I can *undress* for you." As she eased up from the mattress, her hips thrust against his.

He groaned and bit his lip. Then she lifted the sweatshirt over her head and tossed it onto his coat. He groaned again as her breasts jiggled, the nipples peaked toward him. He lowered his head, and his lips closed around one taut point. First he stroked it with his tongue, then his teeth gently nipped.

Erin moaned, and clutched his hair, holding his mouth against her. His fingers stroked her side before tracing the curve of her other breast, his thumb flicking across the taut nipple. She lifted her legs, wrapping them around his hips, straining closer. Still they wore too many clothes. She uttered his name as a plea, begging for more.

But he took his time, driving her slowly out of her mind with desire. She tugged at his shirt, pulling up the cotton until it bared the rippling muscles of his back and chest. Finally he lifted his head from her breast, and she pulled off the shirt.

She gasped at the masculine perfection of his chest and arms. "You're beautiful," she murmured as the overhead light cast a glow across his sculpted muscles. "Golden boy…"

He chuckled. "I used to hate when you called me that…but I could never hate you, as much as I tried."

"Kent…" Tears of regret burned her eyes. She'd treated him so unfairly, but now she wanted to treat him well. Really well. She pushed him back onto the bed and straddled him.

He grinned, but it faded as her lips skimmed across his chest and her tongue flicked his flat male nipple. The point hardened. She skimmed her fingertips across his skin, then down over his navel and washboard abs to the buckle of his belt.

A breath hissed out between his parted lips. He uttered her name as a warning, one she didn't intend to heed. She fumbled with the snap at his waist, then the tab of the zipper. His hand covered hers, stopping her. "Are you sure?"

She answered him with a kiss as she crushed her breasts against his bare chest. His palms skimmed down her back to the waistband of her pajama bottoms, which he pushed over her hips along with her panties. He flipped her suddenly, placing her beneath him again, but he didn't stay on top. He rose from the bed, dropping his jeans and briefs and kicking off his shoes, so that he was naked, too.

Seeing the long, hard, impressive length of him, Erin emitted a quiet whimper. "It's been…a while for me," she admitted. There had never been anyone like him.

He smiled. "For me, too."

She doubted he spoke the truth, but she appreciated the sentiment. "Is it okay…with the bullet?"

"It's okay," he assured her as he pulled a foil packet from his wallet. Instead of tearing open the condom, though, he dropped it on the bed and leaned over her, touching her lips with his in butterfly-soft kisses.

Erin reached out, trying to tug him down on top of her, but he resisted, his biceps bulging as he braced his palms on the mattress on either side of her. Slowly he moved down her body, running his lips along her throat, over the curve of her breasts, down the dip of her navel. And lower.

She rose up, startled. "Kent!"

He soothed her with his hands, stroking her body as he kissed her intimately. She closed her eyes as he made love to her, the pressure winding tight inside her until it broke free. She shuddered, trembling with the aftershocks, but it wasn't enough. She was greedy for more.

He ripped open the condom packet, and moments later, slid inside her. She arched her back and lifted her hips, taking him deep when she had thought they would never fit.

A groan rippled from his throat. "Erin…"

She opened her eyes, meeting his intense gaze.

"You are so beautiful, so perfect…" he murmured.

She wasn't perfect; she'd made so many mistakes. But she could make it up to him. Meeting his thrusts, she nipped at his shoulders with first her nails, then her lips. She nibbled on the cords straining in his neck as he moved in and out of her. Skin slid over skin, heat rising between them as their passion built. And broke. She came apart in his arms, screaming his name.

He tensed, that grimace crossing his face again. This time she didn't feel his pain, though—she felt his pleasure as he thrust deep one last time and came.

ERIN AWOKE, wrapped tightly in Kent's strong arms. She had never felt so safe and protected. And thirsty. The man had exhausted her, making love to her a second time last night. Loving her even more completely.

She licked her lips, but it wasn't enough to quench her thirst. Regretfully, she wriggled free of his hold and slipped from the bed, but tripped over the clothes they'd discarded next to it. This time he wasn't there to catch her when she fell.

Paper rustled as she landed on his leather jacket. A folded file slipped from the pocket, scattering papers atop the rest of their clothes. As she reached to pick them up, she recognized the report number on the side of the documents. Mitchell's arrest record.

"Damn," a deep voice murmured.

Erin glanced up from the papers she clutched, meeting his gaze as he leaned over the bed, staring down at her. "You brought my brother's arrest record and trial transcripts into my *home?* What were you trying to prove?"

He released a ragged sigh. "I was mad…about your last column. When you said you wanted to talk, I thought maybe it was time that you listened."

Tears stung her eyes, but she proudly blinked them back, refusing to cry in front of him—to reveal to him how betrayed she felt. "I don't care what you show me. I'm not going to doubt my brother." Any more than she already had. Which man was telling her the truth? The one she had loved her whole life—or the man she feared she was in danger of falling in love with?

"You're loyal—that's one of the things I find so attractive about you," he said, "but you're also smart, too smart not to question your brother's story."

"Is that why you slept with me?" she asked. "So that I'd fall for you and start giving you good press?"

"You still think that little of me?"

She didn't know what to think, her mind was so muddled and confused. "You're trying to mess with my head." And her heart. Even if it wasn't part of his plan, she was falling for him.

"I'm trying to make you face and accept the truth."

"What *you* claim is the truth."

He drew in a deep breath, as if bracing himself. "Your brother had too many drugs in his possession for the evidence to have been planted. He was dealing, Erin, out of that apartment where Jason was living."

"No!" she screamed. "You're lying."

At that moment, seeing the devastation draining all the color from her beautiful face, Kent wished he *was* lying. "I'm so sorry, honey…."

"About what?" she wailed. "Isn't this what you wanted? You found out my very last secret. Of course you'd want to gloat about it."

"I've known for a while now," he admitted. "That's why I've been avoiding you. I didn't want to tell you. I know you want to believe that your brother is still that boy you idolized growing up."

"And instead you want me to believe that you're the real hero," she scoffed.

That was the last thing he'd wanted. "I just want you to believe *me*."

She shook her head and tears trailed down her face. "I can't…."

He nodded, everything suddenly clear to him. "You'd rather think I'm the bad guy. You'd rather think the worst of *me* than accept the truth."

"My brother swears you framed him," she said, her voice full of emotion. "That you planted that evidence in his apartment."

"Why would I do that?" he asked. "I didn't want my 'promotion.' All I ever wanted was to do my job."

"You're competitive," she cried. "You wanted to do that job better than every other officer."

He wanted to pull her into his arms and comfort her, but he knew she wouldn't let him touch her now. All he could offer her was the truth. "I vowed to protect and serve Lakewood. I would never break the laws I promised to uphold."

She stared at him, almost hopefully, as if she wanted to believe him. But then she shook her head, rejecting his explanation.

"You can't take my word over the word of a *drug dealer?*"

"No…"

He closed his eyes, feeling a spasm of pain, but this one was in his heart, not his back. "I was only doing my job, Erin. Nothing more, nothing less…"

He grabbed his clothes from the floor, dressing hurriedly, desperate to get away from her before she noticed how much she'd hurt him.

"Don't you want this?" she asked, holding out the folder toward him.

"I only wanted one thing from you, Erin."

Her breath caught. "You admit it."

His jaw snapped as he clenched it. "God, you're determined to think the worst of me. I only wanted your trust." And her heart. He admitted that to himself, but couldn't admit it to her.

"Oh…"

"I think you need to take a look at that file and really read it this time," he advised.

"You just want me to change my mind about you," she said, "so I'll stop writing about you."

"I don't care anymore," he stated, and wished he really meant it. "I realize this was a mistake, getting involved with you. You don't trust me, and I sure as hell shouldn't have trusted you."

Every muscle ached as he forced himself to turn away from her, to leave her sitting on the floor clutching that folder. “I’m sure I’ll be reading about tonight in your next column.” He dragged a hand through his hair. “No, actually, I’m done reading your byline. I’m just done….”

Chapter Thirteen

"YOU CAME BACK TO VISIT pretty soon. Is something going on with Jason?" Mitchell asked through the phone clutched to his ear.

"Jason's fine," she assured him, except that he now idolized the man who'd put his father in jail. "He's actually doing really well." Dropping him off at school was no longer the emotional scene it had been. Instead of crying and claiming to be too sick to leave her, he waved and headed off to join his friends.

"You're not fine. You look like hell, sis," Mitch said with a grin to soften the insult. "What's going on?"

She paused, bracing herself to ask him what she had to know. "I need the truth."

Through the glass, Mitchell's gaze met hers, his brow furrowing with confusion. "Erin—"

"I'm not your little sister anymore." That child who had followed him everywhere, who had worshipped him because he'd paid her the attention her parents hadn't spared them. "I'm all grown up now, Mitch."

He smiled, although it didn't brighten his eyes. "I don't know when that happened. When I left for college or when you left..."

"It doesn't matter," she said with a shrug. "I just want you to know that I can handle the *truth*."

"The truth?"

"I want you to tell me what *really* happened," she persisted. "Why you're *really* in here."

"You don't believe me?" he asked, looking shocked.

She ignored the pang of guilt that washed over her. She never wanted to hurt him, but if he was lying to her, he obviously had no compunction about hurting her. "Tell me the truth, Mitchell."

"Mom and Randall get to you?"

"No. You know they didn't." She'd always taken his side over theirs, even when she probably shouldn't have. Growing up, she had lied for him, covering when he'd missed curfew or skipped classes.

Mitchell shook his head. "Damn. Damn. Damn. *He* did. Terlecki got to you."

Anger rushed through her that he continued to avoid answering her question.

"Forget it," she said. "I don't need to hear it from you. I'm a reporter. I'll find out everything I need to know on my own."

She started to hang up the phone.

"Wait!"

"Wait for what?" she asked. "More lies?"

"I'll tell you the truth." He slumped in his chair, defeated.

And so was Erin. She didn't even need to hear his story to know it. She'd already read it in Kent's report and the trial transcripts. When she'd first moved to Lakewood, she had dug up abbreviated versions of both, but she hadn't seen the full details. She realized now that she hadn't wanted to know the truth then.

"I belong in here," Mitchell admitted. "I'd been dealing since college. That's why I got expelled."

She'd thought he'd dropped out; that was what he'd originally told her. Not only had he had her lie *for* him, he'd lied *to* her. Again and again. She closed her eyes against the sting of tears.

In her mind she'd made a man a hero who was really anything but—and in articles and her column she'd vilified the man who was the true hero.

"My arrest was probably well overdue," Mitchell confessed, with another sigh, this one of relief, as if he was actually glad to admit the truth finally. "I'd been dealing for a while, even had people under me."

Kent's report had claimed that Mitchell was midlevel, but wouldn't give up those he was working for. "Why?"

He shrugged. "I don't know. It snowballed, you know? I started using, but I couldn't pay for it. Randall had cut me off when I got expelled."

"That's why you did it," she realized. "To get back at Mom and Dad."

He snorted. "Hell, probably, yes. I guess I wanted to screw up the little perfect lives they thought they had, that they really wanted everyone else to think they had."

"You really screwed up your own life," she pointed out. "And Jason's..."

A tear slipped down Mitchell's cheek, but he brushed it away with his fist. "So that's it, Erin. The *truth.* Is that what you wanted to hear, sis?"

"No," she said. "That's why I never pressed you before. I guess I always knew. I wanted you to still be my hero."

Mitchell sighed. "I never deserved your respect, Erin. I've never been the guy you thought I was—the guy you wanted me to be. I wish I was."

"You're that guy right now," Erin assured him.

He shook his head and gestured around the prison. "I'm in here. Good guys don't go to jail."

"That's not what Sergeant Terlecki told Jason," she shared, remembering her nephew's relief at Kent's answer.

Color drained from Mitchell's face. "Terlecki talked to Jason?"

"Kent spoke at Jason's school assembly." For a guy who hated his new job, Kent had been so good with the kids. "Your son asked him if only bad guys go to jail."

Another tear slipped down Mitchell's face and he sniffled. "Oh, God…"

"Kent told him no," she said. "He told him that good people can go to jail, too, just because they made some bad mistakes."

Mitchell pushed a shaking hand through his dark hair. "I made a lot of bad mistakes, sis."

"I know. I hate what you did—what you *were*." A drug dealer. The thought made her physically ill. "But I don't hate you."

"You're too good-hearted for me to lose your love," Mitchell said, "but I know I've lost your respect."

"Actually, I don't think I've ever respected you more than I do now," she replied. "Thank you for finally telling me the truth."

"I was afraid to tell you," he said. "Afraid that you wouldn't come around anymore. The guys in here that get no visitors—they have no reason for living."

"You're going to keep getting visitors," she promised, lifting her palm to the glass.

Mitchell pressed his against it. "You're *my* hero, Erin. I hope you find someone worthy of you."

She had, but she hadn't been worthy of *him*. And because she hadn't trusted him, she had lost him.

"WELL, THIS IS KIND OF awkward," Mitchell Sullivan commented through the phone pressed to Kent's ear.

"Yeah." Kent didn't often make the trip to the prison on the far east side of Lakewood to visit people he'd arrested.

"My sister told me I'd keep getting visitors," Sullivan said as he leaned back in his plastic chair on the other side of the glass, "but somehow I didn't think she was talking about *you*."

"She wasn't." And she probably wouldn't be too damn happy to learn Kent had visited her brother.

"So you two aren't talking?" Mitchell asked. "Is that why she looks like hell? You've been giving her a hard time?"

"You get the paper in here," Kent said. "I think you know who's been giving who the hard time."

Mitchell laughed. "My little sister can be quite the pit bull when she's defending someone she loves."

"Yeah, she loves you." Selfishly, Kent wished she loved him, or at least trusted him. But that wasn't fair, when he had nothing but uncertainty to offer her. "She shouldn't have found out the truth about you from me." Especially not from papers she'd picked up from her bedroom floor.

Mitchell sighed. "No, you're right, but, man, you don't know Erin—"

"I know Erin." After making love with her, he knew every inch of her body and her heart.

"You know the Erin she is now," her brother explained. "You know the Erin she became to defend me."

"The pit bull."

"You don't know what she was like before," he said wistfully. "The girl who was in the Peace Corps, who wanted to save the world."

"The one who takes care of your son, who loves him as fiercely and protectively as if she were his mother," Kent finished. "Yeah, I know that Erin, too."

Mitchell Sullivan narrowed his eyes, as if struggling to see through the glass. "It sounds like you more than know her. You've fallen for my little sister." He laughed again, but this time without humor. "Now *that's* awkward."

"It's impossible." For so many reasons.

Mitchell shrugged. "Maybe not. I think she actually has feelings for you, too."

Kent suspected as much, or she wouldn't have made love with him in the first place. "It'd be better for her if she didn't."

The other man shook his head. "Yeah, I'd rather she fell for someone who hadn't put me behind bars."

Kent opened his mouth.

Mitchell held up a hand. "I know. You were just doing your job. Unfortunately for me, you're damn good at it."

"I don't have that job anymore," Kent said, and for once frustration and regret didn't overwhelm him that he didn't.

"I heard," Mitchell said. "You got promoted."

"I got *shot,*" Kent admitted. "Couldn't be out in the field anymore."

Sullivan's eyes widened in surprise. "That probably made a lot of criminals happy."

"Probably."

"But not you."

"No." Kent shifted on the hard plastic chair and winced.

"You're still hurting," the other man observed. "When'd you get shot?"

"Three years ago."

"Sheesh." Mitchell snorted. "You must have had a quack for a surgeon."

He'd find out soon enough; he'd made an appointment with a new specialist. "I don't know. I just know your sister deserves someone *whole*—someone she won't wind up taking care of."

"She deserves someone who loves her." Mitchell sighed with resignation. "And I think you do."

"No, I don't." He couldn't love her and risk becoming another burden for her. "But I didn't come here to talk about Erin."

"You didn't?"

"No." He didn't even want to *think* about her, but he couldn't get her out of his mind. His body hadn't stopped aching for wanting hers again.

"Well, I don't know what you and I have to talk about besides Erin," Mitchell pointed out. "Especially since the last time we *talked,* I wound up in here."

"Let's talk about getting you out."

Mitchell's mouth dropped open in shock and disbelief. Then understanding crossed his face. "Wow. You *really* love her."

"This isn't about Erin. This is about you finally giving me the information I wanted when I arrested you."

"The names."

Kent nodded. "I don't understand why you wouldn't before. You could have gotten your sentence reduced."

"Jason."

"He'll be safe," Kent assured him.

"And Erin. She won't get hurt?"

"Not by anyone you give me."

Mitchell shook his head. "I kicked myself a hundred times over the past four years, wishing I had told you, thinking it was too late."

"It might be," Kent admitted. "But if the names lead to more arrests, I know a prosecutor who'll go to the judge and the parole board on your behalf."

Actually Paddy knew the prosecutor best, but Kent wasn't sure if asking the watch commander to go to Anita Zerfas would help or hurt Mitchell's chances for early parole. Paddy and Anita had a complicated history, but Kent's reason for persuading Mitchell to give up the names wasn't to get him out, it was to make Mitchell the hero Erin had believed her big brother to be.

"Erin told me what you told my son, about good people making mistakes."

"He's a great kid."

"Because of Erin." Sullivan's throat moved as he swallowed hard. "Whenever I get out, I'm not taking him away from her. She's his mother now. Jason belongs with her."

Kent nodded, and finally he saw why Erin had idolized her big brother. He was a better man than Kent had given him credit for being.

"I'll give you the names," Mitchell said, "but it's okay if I serve the rest of my sentence. A man needs to pay for his mistakes." Obviously Mitchell, too, wanted to finally earn his sister's respect.

Kent nodded.

"If you let Erin go," Mitch added, "you're going to pay for it."

"You're threatening me?" he asked, amused by the protective-older-brother routine.

"No, I'm warning you. If you build up walls to keep her out, you're putting yourself in prison, man. And it's a lonely place to be."

Kent silently agreed. Life without Erin would seem like prison, but her having to take care of him would be like giving her a life sentence she'd done nothing to deserve.

Chapter Fourteen

Kent was speaking, but Erin couldn't hear the words, with the sound of blood rushing through her head. Three weeks had passed since she'd seen him last, since he'd walked away from her.

Of course, she had seen him on the news, being the face everyone saw at scenes of accidents and crimes, but she hadn't been in the same room with him, close enough to touch him, the way she'd touched him that night.

Until now.

He sat on the edge of the officers' table, his long legs stretched out before him. If Erin stretched, she might be able to touch her toe to his, the thought of which quickened her pulse.

She lifted her gaze to his face. Those mesmerizing gray eyes stared at her. He had never looked at her so coldly before, not even when she'd written those awful columns about him. Heat rushed to her face as shame filled her. She needed to tell him she was sorry, but he refused to take her calls. She couldn't blame him, though, not after she'd believed the worst of him.

She owed him more than an apology. She owed him

a retraction, but Herb had flat out threatened to fire her if she didn't continue writing her columns in the same tone. Since the *Chronicle* was the only paper in town, she'd applied at a couple of the network affiliates in Lakewood, but they'd laughed at her idea of reporting. In trying to ruin Kent's career, she'd actually ruined her own, or at least her chance of ever becoming the credible journalist she'd once longed to be.

Breaking eye contact with her, Kent cleared his throat and addressed the CPA. "Tonight's class is about an officer's worst nightmare—a hostage situation. Hostage negotiator Lieutenant Marilyn Horowski and SRT member Sergeant Sean O'Donnell will discuss a couple of past examples, and how and why they took the steps they did to handle them."

Someone behind Erin gasped, and she glanced back and noticed one of the young teachers' faces had drained of all color and her mouth gaped open in shock. Erin wasn't surprised now that the department would so openly share this information. After all, through the Freedom of Information Act it was available to the public. Also, the Lakewood Police Department had nothing to hide. The only secret they had tried to keep from the community was Kent's injury, and she suspected that had been his decision. Probably his first one as Lakewood's public information officer.

"Our goal is to get everyone out of the situation safely," Kent said. "We don't want anyone getting hurt."

Erin closed her eyes. He'd not only gotten hurt in the line of duty, she had hurt him with her scathing articles and snarky column.

"I'll leave the rest for the experts to explain," he said

as he stood up. Instead of taking his empty chair behind it, he headed toward the door at the back of the room.

Erin slipped out of her seat and followed him into the hall. "Kent!" She had to run to catch up with his long strides. "Kent!"

He stopped at the elevator and turned back to her, his gaze still aloof and impersonal. It was as if he'd never seen her naked, as if he'd never kissed every inch of her bare skin.

Suddenly chilled, she shivered.

"You're missing the class, Ms. Powell."

"I'd rather talk to you." Somewhere private, where she could tell him and *show* him how sorry she was.

"You'll have to wait until the department's next press conference," he said. "I have an appointment."

"It's six-thirty," she pointed out, then tried to warm him up with a smile. "Aren't most appointments between nine and five?"

"You're going to make me say it?" he asked with a heavy sigh.

"Say what?"

"I have a date."

She sucked in a breath of surprise. "Okay. Don't let me keep you then." She whirled away from him and, blinded by a haze of tears, walked back to the conference room. But she hesitated before stepping inside.

"You okay?" a female voice asked.

Erin blinked to clear her eyes and focused on the dark-haired police officer standing in front of her. "Uh, Officer Meyers?"

The woman nodded.

Erin searched her memory for what she'd heard about the young vice cop. Despite her small stature, Roberta Meyers was tough and ambitious. Rumor claimed that she was trying to surpass Sergeant Terlecki's arrest record. Was she the officer about whom Reverend Holden Thomas had spoken? Somehow Erin suspected she was.

"Are you okay?" Officer Meyers repeated her earlier question.

"Yes." She drew in an unsteady breath. "Yes, I'm fine." She cocked her head and studied the woman. "I'm surprised you would care enough to ask, though. I'm not very popular around here."

"I know."

"So you're just doing your job," Erin said, "checking on me?"

"According to Joelly Standish, you're just doing *your* job," Roberta said. "If you didn't write the articles and column the way you do, you'd get fired."

"How do you know that?"

"Joelly and I go back a long ways," she admitted. Before Erin could ask about the odd friendship, Roberta continued, "And I'm not asking as an officer. I'm asking as a woman." A woman who was apparently having some romantic issues of her own.

"Thanks," Erin said.

Roberta glanced toward the elevator Kent had taken. "Sergeant Terlecki is really a great guy."

"I know." She stared wistfully at the elevator door. "I was wrong to write the articles I have."

"Great guys—guys you can *trust*—they're really hard to find," Roberta remarked.

Erin nodded. "I know." But she had lost her chance with Kent, and he wasn't willing to give her another one, not even to apologize.

"SO WHAT DID YOU LEARN?" the chief asked as he poked his head inside Kent's office.

Not to fall in love. It hurt worse than the bullet in his spine. He'd had to fist his hands to keep from touching Erin, especially after he'd lied to her about having a date. Yet no one knew better than he did how persistent she could be; he'd had to hurt her to get her to leave him alone.

But that look on her face, that flash of pain that darkened her brown eyes, haunted him. He had to struggle to stay at his desk, to stop himself from returning to the conference room and telling her the truth.

"Kent?" the chief prodded.

Deliberately misunderstanding, he said, "I didn't stick around for the class tonight. I just introduced Mom and Odie." He referred to Lieutenant Marilyn Horowski and Sergeant Sean O'Donnell by their department nicknames.

"I'm not talking about the CPA, and you know it," Frank Archer said, his blue eyes narrowed. "I know you went to the surgeon this week."

"There are no secrets around here, huh?" Damn, Billy had a big mouth, although Kent wasn't sure how his roommate had found out about the doctor's visit. Neither of them had been around the house much lately, but Kent had clipped the appointment card to the fridge with a magnet.

"Oh, I don't know about that," Frank mused as he leaned against the doorjamb, his head ducked so his salt-

and-pepper hair just brushed the top of the frame. "I think everyone has a secret or two."

Kent studied his boss's face. Kent had been so wrapped up in his own stuff that he hadn't been paying much attention to his friends. Only God, and probably his mother, knew what Billy was doing. And now the chief…

Concern filling him, he asked, "Is there something going on with you?"

Frank shook his head. "We're talking about *you*—your secrets. You've managed to keep a few from Ms. Powell."

Kent leaned back in his chair again. "She knows pretty much everything now."

"About the shooting?"

"Not the details." He didn't know if he could trust her with the particulars. "But she knows I was shot."

"Hmm, maybe she's a better reporter than I thought," he said, then snorted derisively. "No, she's still writing that drivel."

"She may not have a choice." Not if she wanted to keep a roof over her and Jason's heads.

"What do you mean?"

"Her boss is Herb Stein, remember?"

The chief muttered a curse under his breath. "The mayor's puppet."

"Yup. And he's probably pulling Erin's strings, too." Kent wanted to believe that she wouldn't willingly continue to write about him the way she had.

"You don't know that for sure, Kent," Archer pointed out. "You're giving her more credit than she's probably due."

"If you've read her last few columns, you'll see she's tried to focus more on the CPA."

"Yet there was always some article mentioning your latest press conference," the chief reminded him. Then he shook his head. "Damn, you've done it again."

"What?"

"You distracted me from the original question." The chief laughed. "Maybe she is right about you. You're too good at your job."

Kent couldn't suppress a grin. "I've gotten used to it."

"Yet you want to go back in the field."

He'd once thought so; he'd thought that was all he wanted. Now, Erin was all he wanted. "No, I just don't want to be in a wheelchair."

"So you're not having the surgery."

"Actually, I am," he admitted. "I should have talked to you first, made sure someone could cover my time off, but I already scheduled it."

Frank came around Kent's desk and settled onto a corner of it. Then he reached out, squeezing Kent's shoulder in support. "I don't care how much time you need off—you've got it. I care about you. The risk you're taking…"

Kent shrugged. "Is slightly less than it was three years ago."

"Only *slightly?*" Concern filled the chief's blue eyes. "So there's still a chance that you could be paralyzed?"

"If I have the surgery," he said. "If I don't, scar tissue's going to keep building up, causing nerve damage that could lead to paralysis anyway."

"God, man!" He closed his eyes. "So you're damned if you do…"

"Damned if I don't." Either way, the risk was too great to admit his feelings to Erin. If she knew how he felt, she would stick by him as she had her brother and her nephew. And Kent couldn't add to her burdens.

"I'M GLAD YOU CAME ALONG tonight," Marla Halliday commented as she led Erin back to the game area at the Lighthouse.

Actually, Erin had been the one to suggest they play darts. After the way she'd treated Kent, she wouldn't mind hurling a few sharp jabs into her own face. "Really?" she replied, questioning the woman's seemingly sincere welcome.

"It's been a few weeks since you've stopped by after class," the older woman said as she handed over the darts.

Erin managed a smile. "I didn't think I'd be missed."

"You have to understand why everyone's given you a hard time," Marla said, with more commiseration than censure now. "But Joelly Standish joined us one night after class, and she explained about her father and the chief. She doesn't think you have a choice about the articles you write. Neither does Tessa, who told us about your nephew, how you're responsible for taking care of him."

Heat flushed Erin's face. She didn't deserve the woman's change of heart. "In the beginning writing those articles was my idea," she admitted with a sigh. "But I was wrong about the department."

"And Kent."

Especially Kent. "Unfortunately, my boss won't let me write a retraction. He won't let me change the column, either," she said. "And Kent won't even let me apologize."

"Men can be stubborn fools," Marla said, her voice sharp with disgust. "Too damn proud for their own good."

First Tessa, then Roberta and now Marla. Was every woman Erin knew having romantic issues? Some of the pressure eased from her chest, since she didn't feel quite so alone with her problems. Morbidly happy at the thought, she lifted her gaze to focus on the dartboard. "My picture's gone."

Marla nodded. "Kent took it down himself some weeks ago. I don't think he ever appreciated Billy putting it up for him. No matter how vicious you were to him, the man always had a soft spot for you."

"Not anymore." She glanced toward the bar, where he sat with his date—the Channel 7 reporter.

"You know, even when I was disgusted with you for writing those articles, I still admired you," Marla confessed.

Brow furrowed in confusion, Erin turned back to the other woman. "How?"

"You had guts to take on the department, to take on Sergeant Terlecki." Marla gestured to where he sat, his blond head bent close to the reporter's red one. "I thought you were a fighter."

Erin shook her head in self-disgust. "I was fighting the wrong battle then."

"So go fight the right one," Marla advised. "Fight for the guy you want."

"I..." Couldn't deny that she wanted Kent. "You're right."

Marla took the darts from her hand, perhaps not trusting Erin with them around Monica Fox. "Go..."

Erin had to smile. Just a few weeks ago, the woman

had been telling her to go, but for another reason. "Thanks."

Marla nodded, and murmured, "Now if only I could take my own advice..."

Erin wanted to ask her new friend what was bothering her, but Marla planted a hand on her back, pushing her toward the bar. Despite the nudge, Erin walked slowly toward Kent and his date, uncertain what to say now, when she had always had so many words. Too many words.

He didn't turn toward her, but he obviously tensed, as if aware of her presence. She raised her voice above the din of the crowd and said, "Excuse me."

The reporter flicked her an irritated glance and reached out, putting her hand over Kent's, where it rested on the bar. She stroked her long, red nails over his skin with all the subtlety of a dog marking its territory.

Erin barely resisted the urge to shudder. She ignored the woman and focused on Kent. "I need to talk to you."

"I'm off duty," he said, which was obvious, since he wore faded jeans and his leather jacket instead of his uniform.

"It's not the department I want to talk to you about," she said, then swallowed hard. "I want to talk about us."

He shook his head and tossed back words at her that she had uttered to him so long ago. "There is no us, Ms. Powell."

Monica Fox's painted lips lifted in a triumphant smile, while Erin's heart clenched with pain.

"I—I just wanted to apologize," she murmured thickly, through the tears burning her throat.

"It's too late," Kent said.

Erin nodded in agreement and turned away, pushing blindly through the crowd.

Maybe he wasn't the man she'd thought he was, after all. Or maybe he was. Just a man, not the *great* man Roberta had claimed him to be. Even though he was a hero, he was still human. A man who'd slept with her and then moved on to another woman. He was a user.

Now he wouldn't even accept her apology. Erin had nothing left to give him but her heart, and apparently he didn't want that.

Chapter Fifteen

"I'm sorry," he said the minute she pulled open the door, but his apology didn't clear the pain from her dark eyes. That wounded look had haunted him since she'd run out of the Lighthouse an hour ago, and he'd known he would get no rest until he saw her again.

"For what?" she asked through the mere crack she'd opened.

"You're not going to let me in?"

She shook her head. "Jason's sleeping."

"Your mom didn't take him tonight?"

"She only did that the once."

The night they had made love.

"She didn't realize how much work it was to get him ready for school the next morning."

Work that Erin did every morning by herself.

"Then there was the long drive to bring him to school. It didn't work out," she said.

That hurt flickered in her brown eyes again, and Kent knew she wasn't talking about just her nephew spending the night. *His* spending the night with her hadn't worked out, either.

"I'll keep my voice down," he promised, not waiting for her to agree before he shouldered open the door and brushed past her, his chest bumping hers.

She sucked in a breath and stepped back, closing the door behind him. "Breaking and entering," she murmured.

"I didn't break anything," he protested. But then he wondered—had he broken her heart? Could she care about him as much as he cared about her?

He'd wanted to step back from her so he wouldn't cause her more grief with his medical issues, but he was afraid that he'd failed. He walked into the living room, not trusting himself to remain in the close confines of the foyer with her and not touch her, not kiss her. It was good that Jason was home.

Kent noticed the open laptop casting light on the pillows of the couch. "So are you writing about what a jerk I am?" he asked.

Her face bright with color, she stepped around him and closed the computer.

"It's okay," he assured her. "This time I probably deserve it."

"I'm surprised you're here," she replied.

"I know I've been avoiding you." He couldn't tell her why, though. He had been crazy to come here. And selfish.

"I thought you were on a date," she said, her voice sharp with bitterness. Was it possible she was jealous?

He grinned, ridiculously pleased that she cared. "I wasn't on a date."

"That's not what you told me."

"I lied. I spent your class time in my office, working." Getting caught up so he could take time off. "Billy called me and asked me to stop by the Lighthouse."

Interestingly, his friend hadn't shown up himself. Being undercover was like that—things unexpectedly arose. Somehow Kent suspected more was going on with his friend than the job, though.

"So you just ran into Monica Fox?" Erin gazed at him.

He nodded. "We weren't on a date."

"She didn't seem to realize that."

"I don't care what she thinks." He stepped closer, unable to stay away from Erin. He ran his thumb along her jaw, then tipped up her chin. "I care what *you* think." And he hadn't been able to let her believe he would go from her arms to those of another woman. He couldn't let her think what he'd seen on her face, that that night they'd spent together had meant nothing to him.

She blinked those thick lashes. "You could have fooled me. I've been trying to talk to you, to apologize…."

"I don't want your apology." He just wanted her. But it wasn't fair to get so deeply involved when he had no idea if he would have a future to offer her.

"But I've been so awful to you," she said, her voice laced with guilt. "I was so wrong…about everything… but most of all about *you.* I'm sorr—"

He pressed his finger across her lips. "I don't need the words. You don't have to tell me. I understand… everything. I know you were acting out of loyalty to your brother."

Embarrassment heated her face, but not as much as his touch. She had missed it; she had missed *him.* "Turns out he didn't deserve my loyalty."

"You love him."

"Yes." She sighed. "Even though I hate what he did, I still love him."

"I admire that about you," Kent said, "that you're going to stick by him."

She furrowed her brow, detecting something in his tone. "Did someone *not* stick by you? Did someone leave you when you got shot?"

He shrugged as if it didn't matter. "They were already gone."

"Who?" Jealousy clutched at her. "A girl?"

"My folks. They weren't too happy when I chose the police academy over the family farm," he admitted.

"What do you mean, they're 'gone'?" she asked. Even though her parents didn't approve of what Mitchell had done, her mother still visited him, and her father probably would if Mitchell would agree to see him.

Kent shrugged again. "I don't know if they officially drummed me out of the family, but we haven't talked in years."

"Not even when you got shot?"

"I told the chief not to call them."

"Kent, they had a right to know." Just as she'd had a right to know when Mitchell had been arrested. Yet her parents had chosen not to tell her until she came home from South America. "You should have called them."

"And hear what? I told you so?" He gave a short, bitter laugh. "They didn't want me to become a police officer."

"But you did anyway."

"Sometimes I feel like I didn't have a choice. I just had to..."

"I misjudged you," she murmured. "I feel so badly about that."

"It's okay," he assured her.

She shook her head. "No—"

"You were being loyal to your brother. That's the way you are," Kent said, with understanding and something that made Erin uneasy—something like resignation or regret. "You don't need to apologize for that, or to me, for anything."

She doubted she could have been as forgiving as he was. "You're not going to let me say the words?"

A slight grin curving his lips, he shook his head. "It's not necessary."

She linked her fingers with his and tugged him toward the hall. "Then let me *show* you how sorry I am."

"But Jason's home," he reminded her as they passed her nephew's room. Kent resisted her efforts to pull him into her bedroom.

"We're going to be very quiet," she promised him. "In fact, we won't be talking at all, since you won't let me say the words."

He chuckled. "Erin..."

"We'll lock the door."

His grin widening, he stepped over the threshold, and Erin closed the door behind him. He chuckled again as she clicked the lock.

"Shh..." she said, but instead of placing her fingers across his lips, she rose up on tiptoe and pressed her mouth there.

He cupped her face and kissed her back.

She pushed his jacket from his broad shoulders, then attacked the buttons on his shirt, parting the fabric to bare his chest for her hands—and her mouth—to explore. His throat rippled as she slid her lips up his neck, to where his pulse pounded with desire for her.

A groan barely escaped him before he bit it back. "Erin, you're killing me."

"I haven't shown you anything yet," she promised as she unclasped his belt and jeans, pushing the denim and briefs down his lean hips. Then she dropped to her knees.

"Erin..." His fingers tunneled through her hair, trying to pull her back up.

She began loving him with her mouth, sliding it down the hard length of his erection. She gazed up at him, at the look of torment on his handsome face.

Done with being gentle, he lifted her from the floor and carried her to her rumpled bed. The sweatshirt, the same ratty gray one she'd worn the first time they'd made love, ruffled her hair as he dragged it over her head, then dropped it to the floor. Next came the camisole she wore beneath it, freeing her breasts.

He teased her the way she'd teased him. Slowly. Sensually. He skimmed her pajama bottoms down her legs, then pulled aside her panties and loved her with his mouth.

Erin grabbed a pillow from the bed, biting a corner of the cotton case to hold in her cries of pleasure as her body writhed and shuddered. Gasping for breath, she reminded him, "I'm supposed to be showing you how sorry *I* am."

He left her for a moment to retrieve his wallet and protection, then joined her on the bed once more. Erin pushed him onto his back and straddled his lean hips. Bracing her palms against the hard muscles of his chest, she eased herself onto him, taking him deep inside her. She threw her head back and moaned at the erotic sensation.

"Shh..." he reminded her, rising up to silence her

with his lips. His tongue moved inside her mouth, mimicking his movements inside her body, thrusting slowly in and out. His hands skimmed over her skin, cupping her breasts, and he stroked his thumbs back and forth across her nipples.

The pressure inside Erin built again, with such intensity that it was almost painful when it broke. His hands clasped her hips, thrusting her up and down. Suddenly, he threw back his head and bit his lip, groaning as he came, too.

Erin collapsed onto his chest, his skin damp with his perspiration and hers. She sighed as his palm moved down her spine.

"That was some apology," he said.

"It's not enough..." She propped her chin on his chest and gazed up into his gray eyes. "I wish I could print a retraction. That I could tell everyone how wrong I was about you."

"Stein won't let you."

"He'll fire me." She shook her head as frustration tightened the muscles their lovemaking had just relaxed. "I should just quit."

"You can't."

She sighed. "No, I can't. Not until I find another job. I'm trying..." She pressed a kiss against his heart, which beat fast and hard beneath her lips. "But I can apologize for every column just like this," she offered.

"Erin..." That same mixture of resignation and regret that had alarmed her before was back in his voice. "I need to explain—"

"Shh," she said, afraid to hear what he wanted to say. "We're not talking, remember?"

Desire brightened his eyes, and he slid his hands down her back to the curve of her hips. "Then what are we going to do...?"

She smiled as she moved. "I'm sure we'll think of something." But Erin really didn't want to think at all. She only wanted to enjoy *everything* she felt for this man.

KENT DIDN'T KNOW what hurt more—leaving Erin lying alone and naked in bed, or his back. He moved slowly down the hall, carrying his shoes. In the living room he settled next to her laptop on the edge of the couch. Gritting his teeth, he leaned over. His muscles tightened and protested the movement as he slid his feet into his shoes. When he reached for the laces, the muscles spasmed, and a curse slipped out of his lips.

"Did you spend the night?" a soft voice asked.

Kent closed his eyes, feeling a wave of regret, then opened them to focus on Jason. The little boy yawned and blinked the sleep from those brown eyes, which were filled with curiosity and trust.

"No, I fell asleep...on the couch," he lied, hoping the child wouldn't notice that the pillows weren't at all scrunched.

"I do that sometimes, too," Jason admitted, "when I'm watching a boring movie."

"Yeah, that's what happened," Kent said. "Your aunt and I were watching a boring movie. I fell asleep on the couch, and she must have gone to bed." Perspiration trickled down his back. With those unblinking dark eyes, the kid would make a great interrogator someday. Kent hated lying to him.

"You should have waked me," Jason berated him. "I

have some good movies. Do you want to watch one now?" Eagerness brightened his eyes.

Kent's heart contracted with emotion for this sweet boy. In his race car pajamas, with his hair all tousled from sleep, he was adorable. And obviously starved for a male role model in his young life.

"No." Kent couldn't be that role model. He couldn't be anything to the boy or his aunt. He needed to explain that to her, but he didn't want to tell her about the surgery. She would probably insist on sticking by him like she had her brother. "You'd better get back to bed."

"I'm not tired anymore," Jason insisted.

Kent smiled and reminded him, "You have school in the morning, and I have to work."

"You're leaving?"

"Yup, I have to go. I need to be at work really early." While he had a few more weeks before the surgery, he needed every hour on the job to rearrange a schedule he hadn't realized was so busy until he had to find people to cover for him.

"Can you tuck me in before you go?" Jason asked, his brown eyes widening hopefully.

Kent gulped. "Sure. Just let me tie my shoes first." Still holding his breath, he leaned forward, the muscles in his back spasming again as he reached for his laces.

"I can do it," the little boy proudly proclaimed. "Aunt E. taught me. Do you want me to tie your shoes?"

"I'd love that," Kent said.

The little boy's hair fell into his eyes as he knelt at Kent's feet. He pulled his bottom lip between his teeth as he concentrated on wrapping one lace around the other.

Kent doubted his shoes would stay tied long, but he smiled and complimented the child. "Great job, little buddy. Thanks a lot."

He fought the grimace from his face as he stood up. While he hated to take drugs, he might actually fill the prescription for new painkillers.

Jason yawned, then lifted his arms up toward Kent. "Can you carry me?"

He didn't have the heart to refuse the boy. Jason slung an arm around his neck, hanging on as Kent walked down the hall toward his room.

"When are you coming over again?" the child asked, as Kent laid him in his bed. "So *we* can watch movies together?"

Kent's hands shook as he pulled the blankets to the little boy's chin. He would love to be part of this kid's life and a part of Erin's, but he couldn't be what they needed—because *he* might need too much. He couldn't have Erin and Jason taking care of him. It wouldn't be fair.

"I'm not going to be able to come around for a while," he said.

The little boy blinked as if fighting back tears. "Are you going away?"

Regret and guilt slammed through Kent. "I'm not going away like..." Like Jason's father and mother. "I'm just going to be really busy."

"With police stuff?"

He nodded.

"Catching bad guys?"

"Something like that."

"My daddy's in jail," Jason said, his brown eyes filling with fear and tears. "Is he a bad guy?"

"No." Kent brushed Jason's hair back from his serious little face. "Remember what I told you at school? Sometimes good people make bad mistakes." But Mitchell was trying to fix that now, to make up for everything he'd done wrong. "That doesn't make your daddy a bad guy."

Relief filled Jason's dark eyes, and he settled into his pillow and fell back to sleep.

"Everybody makes mistakes," Kent murmured.

"You're making one now," Erin said softly from where she stood in the doorway of her nephew's room.

He couldn't argue with her. Limping slightly, he joined her in the hall. "How long were you standing there?" he asked.

"Just long enough to hear about mistakes," she said. Anger flushed her face as brightly as passion had mere hours ago. "So you were just going to sneak out?"

His face heated, too, with embarrassment. "I was going to leave a note." Once he'd figured out what to write, how to back away without hurting her.

"You should have woke me up."

If he had, he wouldn't have been able to leave her. "I wanted to spare us both an awkward conversation."

"You're a coward, not a hero," she accused.

He couldn't argue with that. "I didn't know what to say."

"Goodbye? Thanks? See you later?"

He latched on to the one he least wanted to utter, but he had no choice. He couldn't expect her to stick by him, not with his uncertain future. "Goodbye."

She drew in a sharp breath. "Goodbye?" Her head jerked in a nod that sent that lock of hair tumbling across her cheek. "So you can't forgive me for what I've written about you, for what I believed?"

His heart clenched. The last thing he wanted was for her to blame herself for his walking away. "You thought the worst of me, Erin," he reminded her. "You don't trust me."

"I was wrong." She lifted her chin. "And if you walk away from *this*, from *us*, you're wrong, too."

"Then I guess I'm wrong."

Chapter Sixteen

"As Lieutenant O'Donnell said, I'm pretty sure everyone knows how to lodge a complaint," Kent said with that charming grin that so infuriated Erin. "You can pick up the phone and call, or come down in person to the department."

Erin hadn't done either of those things. Yet. Three weeks had passed since they'd made love.

"And now, Internal Affairs Investigator Lieutenant Wendy Bell will explain the process that happens once a complaint is made," Kent continued, "and she'll explain the difference between a formal and informal complaint."

Like the last time he'd helped introduce a class, Kent didn't take his chair at the officers' table, but headed out the door again. And just like last time, Erin followed him. He moved slower tonight, with the slight limp she had noticed he'd had at her place, and she caught up with him easily.

She ducked in front of him, so that he couldn't step onto the elevator and ignore her. "I'd like to lodge a complaint," she said.

A muscle twitched in his cheek as he stared over her head, as if unable to meet her gaze. "Then you need to talk to Lieutenant Bell."

"It's an informal complaint," she explained, "just between you and me."

He shook his head. "There is no you and me."

She sucked in a breath as if he'd slapped her. "You really can't forgive me?" she asked. "Even now?"

Herb had let up on her at the *Chronicle,* no longer requiring the vindictive tone she'd used when writing anything pertaining to the police department. She suspected Joelly had talked to her father.

"There's just too much between us," Kent said. "I'm always going to be the guy that arrested your brother."

"But I don't blame you anymore," she insisted. "I realize you were just doing your job and that Mitchell was in the wrong."

"It's too complicated between us," he stated, his gray eyes dark with regret. "There's so much hurt and mistrust. But even if there wasn't, I don't have time for a relationship. Because of my job, I can't give you and Jason the attention you both deserve."

"Jason said you'd told him you're going to be very busy." Anger coursed through her as she remembered the disappointment on her nephew's little face. "That's just what the kid didn't need—one more person dropping out of his life."

"I know." Kent rubbed his hand around the back of his neck, as if trying to relieve tension. "I never meant to hurt him."

"Well, you have," she said. "He keeps asking me when you're going to come to dinner again. Or over to watch movies." She blushed as she remembered how Kent had explained his being there late that night. She wanted to "watch movies" with him again. Her body ached for his touch—ached for his…

He lifted his arm as if he couldn't help himself, as if he felt the same way she did. His fingers trembling, he pushed the lock of hair behind her ear, the one that always fell across her cheek.

Her skin tingled from the brief contact with his fingertips. "Kent, tell me what's going on," she implored. "Why you're pulling away…"

She could feel the attraction burning between them, the electricity they hadn't been able to deny even when they'd hated each other. That muscle ticked again in his cheek as he clenched his jaw.

He shook his head. "Like I said, I shouldn't have gotten involved," he repeated. "With either of you. I'm not able to be the man you two need."

Was he like Jason's stepfather? Unwilling to raise another man's son. She suspected he had another reason.

"You really can't forgive me for the things I wrote about you?" she asked doubtfully. He wouldn't have made love with her if he'd been unable to forgive her, but she couldn't blame him if he was still mad. She'd been so unfair. "Herb's loosened up on me, but he won't let me write a formal apology to you."

It killed her that her boss wasn't actually sorry for what they'd done. He was worried about being sued for libel, which he should have considered when he'd been encouraging her to be harsh.

"I don't need one." From his tone, Kent was telling her he didn't need her, either.

He stepped around her and jabbed the button for the elevator, offering her no explanation, just another apology. "I'm sorry."

"Yeah. Me, too." Sorry she had fallen for a man who couldn't love her back. Or who wouldn't allow himself to love her back. Kent Terlecki was no hero.

WITH THE SURGERY ONLY a week away, Kent should have been worried about going under the knife again, but all he could think about was Erin. She hadn't tried to talk to him since that class a few weeks ago—when she had filed her "informal" complaint.

She had every reason to complain. He'd treated her horribly. But maybe someday she would understand that he was trying to protect her, to save her from making any more sacrifices.

Someone slapped a newspaper against his shoulder, where he sat at the bar at the Lighthouse.

"So when are you going to tell her?" Paddy O'Donnell asked as he slid onto the empty stool next to Kent's.

Kent glanced down at the paper Paddy had laid next to his untouched plate of fish, chips and coleslaw. His breath backed up in his lungs at the sight of her picture next to her column, Powell on Patrol. God, he missed her. But the feeling wasn't mutual, if her words were any indication—she'd gone back to calling him a player.

He couldn't blame her. He'd had no right to get involved with her when he'd known he had nothing to offer her.

"Tell her what?" he asked.

"That you're having surgery."

He ignored Paddy's comment. "Thanks for picking

up a lot of the slack when I'm off. I couldn't find anyone but you willing to take on those school assemblies." Even Lieutenant Michalski, who took everyone's extra shifts at the department, had refused. But he'd lost a baby some years ago, and spending time with kids was probably a difficult reminder of that.

Kent turned the paper over, hiding her picture from his sight. It wasn't class night, so she wasn't at the Lighthouse. It was early, too, so she was likely still at work. If there'd been any chance she might have been in the bar, Kent would not have come.

"I like kids," Paddy said, and since his divorce, he didn't see enough of his own children, thanks to the manipulations of his ex-wife.

Kent squeezed his friend's shoulder. "I appreciate it. And I appreciate you talking to Anita Zerfas for me." Thanks to Paddy, Anita had agreed to help reduce Mitchell's sentence for supplying names that had led to several arrests.

Paddy sighed. "I wasn't sure if my talking to her would help or hurt."

Kent didn't know if his friend was referring to Mitchell or himself. "Did it hurt?"

O'Donnell chuckled. "This isn't about me." Talking about Anita had been off-limits for years with Paddy. "We're talking about you, Bullet. Are you ready for the surgery?"

Kent nodded. "Yeah, thanks to all of you helping to cover me at the department."

Paddy shrugged off his gratitude. "Hey, we're all going to be here for you, you know."

"I know." He remembered how everyone had rallied

around him after the shooting. His biological family hadn't been there for him, but the family he'd chosen, the one who mattered most to him, had been.

"She would be there for you, too," Paddy said, flipping the paper back over. "Despite what she writes, I can tell that she cares about you. A lot."

Kent sighed. "I care about her, too."

"So tell her about the surgery," Paddy urged.

"It's *because* I care about her," he explained, "that I don't want her to know."

"THERE'S SOMETHING YOU need to know…."

Erin turned to where Patrick O'Donnell sat behind the wheel of the black patrol car. She still couldn't believe that not only had the watch commander assigned himself to her ride-along, but that he hadn't cancelled it altogether.

Maybe he'd wanted to get her alone to talk. After responding to a couple of calls, one a noise disturbance and the other an alarm going off at a business, O'Donnell had pulled into a park in the suburbs of Lakewood. Since it was late, the park was deserted.

"Here comes the lecture…."

"Here comes the truth."

"I know the truth," she replied as she fiddled with the pages of her open notebook. She'd written down a few notes, but most of the pages were blank. "I know that my brother is really guilty and that Kent is really a hero, that he saved the chief's life."

"He did more than save the chief's life," Paddy said.

"He saved other people, too?" She didn't doubt it, and she wasn't surprised that Kent hadn't mentioned it.

"The woman who shot him," Paddy said. "Kent talked to the district attorney on her behalf."

"On her behalf?" Erin hadn't thought to ask who'd shot him, suspecting it had been difficult enough for him to still have the bullet in his back. "Why would he do that?"

Paddy sighed. "He felt sorry for her."

"But she *shot* him!"

"She'd tried to kill the chief, thinking he'd given the order for the SRT sniper." O'Donnell swallowed hard, as if choking on emotion and regret. "To shoot her son."

"What?"

"You don't know all the details," he realized.

"No. Kent wasn't even the one who told me about the shooting." He hadn't wanted her to know.

"Billy told you."

"Yes."

"It was a hostage situation—a dangerous one. The mother of the suspect didn't appreciate how it was handled. Later, outside the department building, she came after the chief."

"And Kent was the one who got hurt..." Erin closed her eyes, seeing the image of a wounded Kent.

Paddy nodded.

She sucked in a shaky breath. "And he stood up for this woman, anyway."

"That's the kind of guy he is," his friend admitted. "He takes care of everyone...but himself."

"The bullet's bothering him," she mused, remembering the pain on his face, and that Jason had said he'd had to tie Kent's shoes that last night they'd been together.

"Yes," Paddy said. "That's why he's having surgery—to have it taken out."

"What?" Fear clenched her heart in a tight fist. "But isn't there a risk of paralysis?"

Paddy's face paled in the faint glow of the dashboard lights. "I guess that's a risk he's willing to take."

Her fingers trembled against the notepad. "When's he having the surgery?"

"Next week. He scheduled it a while ago."

A while ago? "He never said anything to me." Anger tempered her fear for him; she was so sick of people keeping things from her. First her parents, then Mitchell and Kent.

His voice low and gentle, Lieutenant O'Donnell said, "He doesn't want you to know."

She flinched, hurt that Kent was determined to keep things from her, to shut her out of his life. "But you're telling me despite what he wants."

"*I* think you should know."

"*He* doesn't." She blinked against the scalding tears, unwilling to give in to her hurt feelings. Kent, and the risk he was facing, were more important. And if he didn't want her to be there for him, she had to honor his wishes.

"He doesn't want you to know because he doesn't want to burden you," Paddy explained, reaching over to squeeze her hand. "He's used to taking care of everyone else—the whole damn department. He doesn't want anyone taking care of him—especially someone he loves."

She closed her eyes, afraid to hope, only to have that hope crushed again. "He *loves* me?"

"If he didn't, he would have told you," Paddy said matter-of-factly.

She wasn't convinced of the lieutenant's logic. "Thanks for telling me."

"I thought you had a right to know."

But Kent hadn't. She wasn't certain what to do now. How could she be there for him if he didn't want her?

Lieutenant O'Donnell steered the car out of the parking lot onto a quiet residential street. Erin was grateful for the darkness so that she could wipe away her tears and pull herself together. She was grateful for the silence, needing to think.

Suddenly O'Donnell flipped the switch for the siren, shattering the stillness, before shutting off the siren midwail. Startled, Erin gazed through the window. "What happened? What…"

The lieutenant stared straight ahead, grinning.

Then Erin noticed the vehicles pulled to the side and the man kneeling before the woman in the middle of the street. The blonde flung her arms around the man's neck, holding tight. "Is that…"

"Chad Michalski and Tessa Howard," Paddy said, his deep voice vibrating with satisfaction as his grin widened. "Yes, it is."

Despite what she'd just learned about Kent, Erin's lips lifted in a smile, too. "Is he…"

"Proposing? He damn well better be." He pulled the car next to the surprised couple and rolled down Erin's window. "Everything all right here?" he asked.

Chad Michalski grinned; Erin couldn't remember ever seeing him that excited before. "Everything's *perfect* here, Paddy," he assured the watch commander.

"Congratulations," Erin said, moved by their obvious happiness.

Paddy chuckled as he drove off, leaving the newly engaged couple alone.

"You're really happy for them," she observed.

"I don't know how much you know about Lieutenant Michalski, but he was married before."

"He's divorced?" she asked, curious now about the man who'd made her new friend that happy.

"Widowed, like the chief," he explained. "His wife died in a car accident. She was pregnant."

Sympathy filled Erin. *That poor man.* "He lost the baby, too?"

O'Donnell nodded. "Chad's been miserable these past four years without them. He never intended to risk his heart again, to risk that kind of loss again."

"But he did." She doubted he could have resisted Tessa. The beautiful woman was a force of nature.

"*He* was brave enough to take a chance on love, Erin," Paddy pointed out.

She smiled at the lieutenant's obvious ploy. "I have an older brother. I realize when I'm being goaded."

"You're a smart woman," he said. "Too smart to give up without a fight."

"I've been fighting with Kent since I joined the *Chronicle* staff a year ago," she reminded him. "I don't want to fight anymore." She just wanted to love him, but he kept pushing her away.

"Then don't fight," the watch commander advised. "Just be there for him. Even though he'd be the last one to admit it, he needs you."

And she needed him. She glanced down at the notebook she'd intended to fill with research for her next column, and she flipped through the blank pages, which were going to stay that way.

"Can I cut my ride-along short?" she asked.

"Sure," Paddy said, his lips curving into another grin. "I can drive you back to the department anytime."

"Now, please." She had somewhere more important to be.

Chapter Seventeen

Hammering at the door awoke Kent from a fitful sleep. Had Billy forgotten his key again? Disoriented, Kent stumbled out of his bedroom and crossed the living room to open the front door.

Erin pushed her way past him, then whirled, slamming her palms against his bare chest. Her dark eyes bright with anger, she shouted, "How dare you not tell me!"

"Tell you what?" he asked, trying to clear his head. Her warm hands against his bare skin distracted him, drawing him back into the dream he'd been having of her…of them making love.

"About your surgery," she replied, her voice now soft with hurt.

"Oh, *that,*" he said, wondering which one of his so-called friends had told her. Then he remembered that she'd been riding along with Paddy tonight. "O'Donnell told you?"

"*He* thought I had a right to know," she said.

"*He* needs to stop meddling in other people's lives," Kent griped. "He thinks that because he's watch commander he can play matchmaker, too."

Kent had actually thought it funny when Paddy had messed with Michalski's life; now he realized he owed Chad an apology.

"He cares about you," Erin said, defending the lieutenant. "And he knows *I* care about you."

He closed his eyes in a rush of emotion. "That's the problem, Erin. I don't want you to care about me."

"I think this might be the first time you've actually lied to me," she mused. "You're happy I care about you, Kent. You're just afraid to care about me."

It was too late for those fears. He already cared about her. Hell, he *loved* her; that was why it was so damn hard to push her away. But he had to—for her sake. He opened his eyes and met her determined gaze. "Erin…"

"You already care about me," she said with a triumphant smile.

He couldn't deny his feelings. "That's why I want you to forget about me. You deserve more than I can give you."

"But I want you, Kent," she said, stepping even closer so barely a breath separated their bodies. "I want *you*."

"Erin…" Maybe it was because he'd been dreaming about her that Kent's resolve weakened. He couldn't fight his feeling for her. Not tonight. Holding her hands to his chest, to where his heart pounded madly with desire for her, he leaned over and kissed her.

He hadn't imagined how soft her lips were, how sweet her mouth. He slid his palms down her back, pressing her against him. A groan tore from his throat.

She pulled back, breathing hard. Her brown eyes were even darker with desire. "Is—is Billy here?" she asked.

He shook his head. "No, we're alone." He knew this

was a bad idea and that he should lead her to the door and make her leave. Instead, he entwined his fingers with hers and tugged her toward his bedroom.

"You have on too many clothes," he protested, as he lifted her sweater over her head and tossed it onto the hardwood floor. She wore a shirt beneath the sweater, one with buttons that were too small for his impatient fingers. So he pulled that over her head, too.

"You don't have on many clothes," she said, trailing her fingers down his bare chest to the waistband of the gym shorts he wore.

His erection strained against the material, pressing against her hips. He groaned at the sweet torture. "Erin…"

His fingers shaking slightly, he undid the clasp of her bra, sliding the straps down her shoulders, letting the scrap of lace fall away. "You are so beautiful," he murmured. "Am I still dreaming?"

She shook her head. "If you are, then we're sharing the dream."

He dipped his head, taking her lips in another deep and consuming kiss. Her tongue darted into his mouth, teasing his. He groaned again and skimmed his knuckles down her bare back.

"You feel so real," he murmured against her lips, which curved into a smile.

She moved her hands to the front of his shorts. "You feel so real, too."

He chuckled at her boldness. But when she slipped her fingers inside his shorts, the chuckle stuck in his throat as desire rushed through him. Impatient for her, he undid her pants and pushed them down her hips. "I have to have you…."

"Yes," she agreed, and stepped out of the rest of her clothes so that she stood naked before him.

"Now," he said, as he tumbled her onto his rumpled bed. He'd been restless, unable to sleep for wanting her.

"Yes." She reached for him.

But he pulled back, then dug through the drawer of his bedside table, looking for protection. With a triumphant "yes," he held up a foil packet.

She took it from him, tore it open and rolled the condom down his shaft. "Now."

With a flash of guilt, he shook his head. "I'm rushing you…."

"You're going too slow."

He made sure she was ready for him, caressing and kissing every inch of her, savoring each soft touch and sweet taste. If the surgery didn't go well, he might never be able to do this again. To love her the way she deserved to be loved.

Tears streaked from the corners of her eyes as she shattered in his arms. "Kent! Now! Please!"

She locked her legs around his hips, and he slid home in her wet heat. Her lips skimmed down his throat, her teeth nipping gently as he thrust in and out. She lifted her hips, matching his rhythm until she came again.

He tensed, then his passion for her exploded.

He slipped from the bed for a few minutes, then returned, to drop down beside her, exhausted.

"Wow…" she murmured, her breasts rising and falling with her erratic breathing. "That was some dream…."

"Some dream," he agreed as he leaned over her, brushing his mouth across hers.

Her lips parted, but before he could deepen the kiss, she murmured, "I want to be there for you."

He shook his head. He couldn't ask that of her. It was too great a sacrifice. He encircled her wrists with his hands and lifted her from the bed. "You need to go home, Erin."

Shock and hurt widened her dark eyes. "No, I want to be with you."

"But Jason…" He should have thought of the boy earlier. Heck, he should have thought of Erin earlier, before he'd made love with her again. Kent hated himself for having been so selfish. He never should have made love with her again, but with the very real possibility of the surgery paralyzing him, he was glad that he had. At least he'd have one more memory of being that close to her. Of being a part of her…

"Jason's with my parents," she said, "he's spending the night."

"But what about getting him ready for school…"

"Tomorrow's Saturday. I can be with you," she offered. "Tonight. All night. Always."

It was the *always* that scared him most, the sacrifice she was more than willing to make. The sacrifice he loved her too much to ask her to make. "No, you can't."

"I know you're worried about what might happen with the surgery," she said, excusing his rejection. "That you're worried that you might be…"

"Crippled," he finished for her, when she couldn't even say the word. "That I might wind up spending the rest of my life in a wheelchair."

"Kent, don't worry. I'll be here for you. I'll be by your side," she promised, "no matter what happens."

His worst fear realized, he closed his eyes. God, he

loved her. And it was because he loved her he couldn't accept her offer. He couldn't burden her.

"That's why I don't want you to stay," he said. "I don't want your pity."

"It's not pity," she protested, her anger returning. "I love you!"

He sighed. "That's too bad." Because before he'd only guessed what he was giving up. Now he knew.

Erin realized he was deliberately pushing her away again, but knowing that didn't make his rejection hurt any less. Feeling too vulnerable naked, she grabbed her clothes from the floor, awkwardly tugging them back on.

He lay on the bed, his arm across his face as if he were falling back to sleep. Or as if he couldn't look at her.

"Don't do this," she pleaded.

"Don't do what? Be honest?" he asked.

"Don't try to protect me," she said.

"To protect and serve, that's the oath every police officer takes," he murmured. "I can't break my oath—not even for you, Erin."

"I don't need protecting," she insisted.

"Yes, you do," he said. "You need protecting from yourself. You keep taking on other people's responsibilities."

"Jason isn't a responsibility. He's a joy. I love him. I love taking care of him." She didn't know what she would do, how she would handle the loss if his mother or Mitchell took him from her. Just as she didn't know how she would handle the rejection if Kent kept pushing her away—especially now, when she knew how much he needed her.

"I don't want you to take care of me," he said, his voice rough with pride.

"You are so damn stubborn," she complained. "And chauvinistic. Why can't I take care of you?"

"Because it would kill me," he said, "to be a burden to you. You deserve more than I can offer, Erin."

Paddy was right. Kent loved her, he was just too proud to admit it.

"I still have my question," she remembered. "The one you promised to answer honestly."

"Erin, it's too late…."

She shook her head, refusing to give up on him. "Do you love me, too?"

"You waited too long," he said. "The expiration date ran out on that question a long time ago."

"Then tell me you don't love me," she challenged him.

He sighed. "It doesn't matter. We have no future, Erin."

Tears burned her eyes, but she blinked them back. She was proud also. Too proud to keep throwing herself at a man who only wanted to share his body with her—not his heart, not his life.

"Fine," she agreed. "I'll leave you alone. I think I was wrong, anyway."

"About what?" he asked, as if helpless to resist his curiosity.

"I don't love you," she said. "I don't even know you."

"You know me."

She shook her head. "You won't let me know you. Time and time again you've kept secrets—important secrets—from me. Things I had a right to know. I thought you were protecting me, like my mom and dad claim they were protecting me when they didn't tell me about Mitchell's arrest while I was in South America."

She swallowed hard, her throat dry. "Then Mitchell…

When he didn't tell me the truth, I figured it was because he was protecting me from disillusionment. And I gave you the same excuse for all the things you've kept from me—that you were protecting me."

She shook her head, thoroughly disgusted with herself and everyone else she cared about. "Now I realize you all were just protecting yourselves."

"Erin..."

"You're the worst," she accused. "You're the most scared to let me get to know you, to let me into your heart. I'm done trying," she said, throwing his words in his face. "I'm just done."

"YOU'RE SURE YOU WANT to do this alone, son?" the chief asked him.

Kent sat up in the hospital bed, waiting for the orderlies to bring him to surgery. He stared at all the faces around him. Almost the entire department was present; he hoped the criminal element wasn't aware of how short-staffed the Lakewood PD currently was.

Even some of the CPA members had shown up to support him. Rafe Sanchez and the youth minister, Reverend Thomas, crowded into the room with the police officers, and Brigitte Kowalczek, the bartender from the Lighthouse. Marla Halliday stood close to the chief's side.

"I'm not alone," Kent said with a slight grin, amused that so many people had managed to fit into such a small room, and touched that they were there for him.

"But the person you want the most to be here isn't," Marla said as she leaned over the bed rail and patted his arm. "Why don't you let me call Erin?"

He shook his head. "No, I don't want her here."

"Liar," the chief muttered.

Selfishly, Kent did. He needed her support, her smiling face, to assure him that he was doing the right thing by going through with the surgery. But calling her, asking her to be here when he had nothing but uncertainty to offer her, would be the wrong thing.

Honestly, he doubted she would come anyway. As she'd said, she was done with him. She hadn't tried to call him again. Hell, she hadn't even written about him since that night.

"I *can't* have her here."

"You can't have this many people in here," a nurse complained as she shoved through the crowd. "You cannot have surgery if your blood pressure or your temperature is too elevated."

They were other reasons it was good that Erin hadn't showed up, since she had a knack for raising both. Hell, he would have to be dead not to react to Erin Powell.

"The surgeon is running behind schedule," the nurse continued as she tightened a blood- pressure cuff around his biceps, "so it's going to be a while yet. You need some quiet time."

If the only thing his friends were going to do was badger him to call Erin, he agreed with the nurse's prescription.

"Only one person can stay with you," she added.

He nodded, not caring, since he couldn't have the one person he truly wanted with him.

Chapter Eighteen

"So did you draw the short straw?" he asked Billy, since his friend was the first to walk back into the room after the nurse had shooed everyone out.

"No, we all agreed that I probably had the best chance of getting through your thick skull."

Kent groaned. "I'm supposed to be having quiet time," he reminded his housemate.

"I'm not going to talk to you." Billy slapped a newspaper against Kent's chest. "You're going to read this."

He shook his head. He couldn't even look at the paper. If he caught a glimpse of Erin's picture, he would weaken and call her, and that wouldn't be fair to her—if she even took his call. He had pushed her away so many times that she was probably too far out of his reach.

"Okay, you stubborn ass, I'll read it to you," Billy said, grabbing the paper. "'Today, Lakewood Police Department's public information officer, Sergeant Kent Terlecki, is undergoing surgery at Lakewood Memorial Hospital. Terlecki is having a bullet removed that's been lodged against his spine for the past three years, when he leaped into the line of fire and saved Chief Archer's life.'"

"Dammit," Kent cursed. "She betrayed me. She knew I didn't want that made public!" Maybe he'd been wrong about her—she wasn't being forced to continue the sensational angle of her column. She chose to do it.

"'The shooter, whose son had been killed earlier that day by police, intended to kill the chief out of revenge.'"

"How the hell did she find out about that?" he asked. "Did you tell her?"

"Shut up and listen." Billy continued, "'The shooter, Mrs. Sherry Ludlowe, is serving out her sentence at a psychiatric hospital instead of in prison due to a deal Sergeant Terlecki himself negotiated on her behalf."

Billy hadn't even known that, and probably not the chief, either. Someone else had talked to the prosecutor with whom Kent had worked out that agreement. "Damn Paddy…"

Billy ignored his outburst and kept reading. "'Ludlowe commented, "Terlecki saved my life the day I nearly took his. If I had shot the chief, I would have turned the gun on myself. He protected the chief that day, he protected me and he continued to do so by keeping quiet about what I had done. My son, having taken his class hostage, had already made enough headlines that day. I understand now why the Lakewood SRT officer had to shoot him, so he wouldn't have hurt those innocent children and their teacher. My son was not innocent. And neither am I. I don't deserve the sergeant's protection, his kindness or his forgiveness. He's a true hero."'"

Kent shook his head. "Erin shouldn't have talked to

Mrs. Ludlowe. She shouldn't have brought up all that pain for her again."

"What about your pain?" Billy asked.

Kent gestured around the hospital room, which was as sterile-looking with its white walls and floor as it probably was. "That's why I'm here."

"And this is why *I'm* here," Billy said. "To make sure you read this part. It's the best, so listen closely."

Kent sighed. If not for the IV in his arm, he might have climbed out of bed to escape Billy.

Suspecting that he was tempted to do just that, Billy laid a hand on Kent's shoulder as if to hold him down. "'Lakewood needs to keep Sergeant Kent Terlecki in their prayers today as he undergoes this risky surgery that could possibly leave him paralyzed. The city owes him a debt of gratitude for protecting us. He is our hero. He is *my* hero.'"

"That was Erin's column? She wrote that?" Kent asked, glancing up at his friend for confirmation.

But a female voice answered, "Yes."

He turned toward the doorway, where Erin stood, and his pulse tripped and his skin heated just in reaction to seeing her. She was so damn beautiful. "I don't think that's going to sell that many papers."

"I don't care about the *Lakewood Chronicle*'s sales or circulation." She stepped forward, approaching his bed. "I care about *you*."

Billy patted his shoulder. "I'm getting out of here before Nurse Ratchet tosses me out for us being one over the room limit."

Kent reached out a hand to stop him, but his friend slipped from his grasp. Before leaving, he stopped next to Erin and pulled her into a quick hug. "Good luck with him." Billy turned back to Kent with a wink. "He's a stubborn ass, you know."

"I know," Erin agreed with a smile at Kent as Billy disappeared into the hall.

"Seriously, you're probably going to get fired over this," Kent said, tightening his grasp around the paper Billy had left on his bed.

Erin detected the real concern in his voice, and her smile widened. He loved her. He was just too much of a stubborn ass—as his friend had said—to admit it. *Yet.*

And she loved him. She hadn't slept at all the previous night for worrying about him and his surgery. He looked so healthy, so strong sitting up in bed. The pale green hospital gown took nothing away from his masculinity.

"Erin, you can't afford to lose your job," he said, his concern all for her and none for himself.

"I'm not going to lose my job," she assured him, covering his hand with hers. "Herb okayed the column or it wouldn't have gone to print."

Kent turned his hand over, entwining their fingers. "How did you manage that?"

"With a little help from a fellow CPA member," she said. "Joelly talked to her dad." In fact, she'd tried a while ago, but she finally got through to him.

Disbelief narrowed his eyes. "Joelly? The mayor's daughter?"

Everyone had been wrong about the heiress. She wasn't the bubble-headed ditz she'd been labeled.

"The mayor approved that article?" Kent persisted.

"Shh…" Erin murmured. "Don't worry about any of that. You're off work now."

"I'm going to be off to surgery soon." He swallowed hard then released her hand. "I don't want you here, Erin."

"That's too damn bad," she said. "I'm not going anywhere…that you're not going. You're stuck with me."

"I could get a PPO," he warned her.

"A personal protection order?" She shrugged. "You could, but then you're going to have to go down to the courthouse and swear out a complaint. You'll miss your surgery."

"Maybe I should," he said.

"You would really get a PPO against me?" She had known he was stubborn, but this was extreme, even for him.

He shook his head and clarified, "Maybe I should change my mind about having the surgery."

"No!" she exclaimed. "For weeks you've been planning to have this. You have all your duties covered at the department. You can't back out now."

"I can back out up until the minute they put me under," he said. "Do *you* want me to?"

Her stomach knotted with nerves and dread as she thought of the risk he was taking. "No. I know how much you hate being desked. If you're doing this to get back in the field, I understand and I support you."

"I don't want to go back in the field."

"You don't?"

"I just realized a little while ago that I actually like my job," he admitted, as if confessing a dirty secret. "And I'm good at it."

"Very good," she agreed.

"Even if I come through this surgery fine," he said,

"I'm going to stay on as the department's public information officer."

"Then why are you having the surgery?" she asked him. "Because of the pain?"

"I can live with that," he said, dismissing the pain even though she suspected it was quite severe. "I've been living with it the past few years."

"Then why would you put yourself through this…" her voice cracked with emotion and fear "…through this uncertainty?"

"There's a risk with any surgery," he said, "but there's a risk to leaving the bullet in, too. My future's uncertain, and I didn't want to live with that. I couldn't ask *you* to live with that."

"What?"

"I decided to have the surgery because of you, Erin," he confessed, "so that I'd know what I could offer you and Jason."

"But you kept pushing me away," she said, tears trailing down her face.

He reached out, rubbing his thumb across her cheek, wiping them away. "I needed to know how I was going to come through the surgery. If I did fine, I was going to try to win you back."

"You don't have to win back what you never lost," she said. "You never lost me, and you never will."

"But if I'm paralyzed—"

She pressed her fingers across his lips. "You won't be. You're going to come through this fine. You have to believe that."

He kissed her fingers and pulled her hand from his mouth. "I'm a cop," he said. "I'm a realist."

"And I'm an idealist. I'll give you balance." She sniffed back the threat of more tears. "And I'll give you my heart. Please take it this time."

"I do love you, Erin."

Then the orderly was in the doorway, clearing his throat. "It's time to take you to the O.R., Sergeant Terlecki."

Erin wanted to ask for a few more minutes, but didn't want to keep him from something he should have had done three years ago. So she stood back and watched as he was wheeled away.

"They took him for surgery," she said when she joined his police family in the waiting room. Not long ago she would have walked into a room with these people and been greeted with nothing but hostility. Now they rallied around her with smiles and pats on the back.

"He'll be fine," Billy assured her—and probably himself. "He's a tough son of a bitch...."

"Are you okay, honey?" Marla Halliday asked, sliding an arm around Erin's shoulders.

She could only shake her head. "I didn't get a chance to tell him I loved him." She'd wanted to say the words again. To make sure he knew she meant them, then and now. No matter what happened.

"He knows," Chief Archer assured her, clutching her last column in his hand. "We all know."

"CAN YOU FEEL THAT?" Dr. Maurer asked as he ran something like a roll of spikes across the sole of Kent's foot.

"Yeah," he said, moving his toes. "I can feel *everything.*" Especially the hand holding his. Erin squeezed his fingers, offering her unwavering support.

"So, Doc?" he asked, but he studied her face rather than the surgeon's. "What do you think? Will I be able to dance pretty soon?"

"Dance?" the doctor and Erin both asked.

"I didn't know you were a dancer," she murmured. Doubt flashed in her eyes.

He squeezed her fingers reassuringly. He had so much to make up to her, and he hoped he had the rest of their lives to do it in. "Not usually. But a man has to dance at his own wedding."

"Yes," Dr. Maurer agreed with a chuckle. "Or you would have an unhappy bride."

Erin gasped. "Bride…?"

Kent focused on the doctor. "So will I?" He held his breath, waiting for the reply—waiting for the certainty that he had lived without for the past three years.

The surgeon nodded. "Oh, yeah, and as determined as you seem to be, I think you could even schedule that dance within the next six to eight weeks."

"What do you think?" Kent asked Erin, after the specialist left them.

"About what?" She stood beside his bed, exactly where she'd been when he'd first opened his eyes after the anesthesic wore off. She hadn't left his side, too loyal to leave him when he'd needed her, even though he'd been too stubborn or too stupid to admit it. He was ready to admit it now.

Emotion choked him, making his voice raspy, "I was asking about the wedding."

Her eyes widened in surprise, as if she had no idea what he was talking about. "What wedding?"

"Ours."

Her heart lurched as it had when he'd first mentioned it, but she pushed aside the hope and happiness for the moment. "Ours?"

His mouth curved in a slight smile. "You know—you and me. I want to marry you, Erin Powell."

"What does marriage mean to you, Kent?" She had to know.

"Love," he said, as if that was all that mattered. "I love you. And I'm pretty sure you love me."

"I do." She sighed. "But that's not enough. I want more."

"Whatever you want, I'll find a way to get it for you."

She smiled and blinked back tears at his earnestness. "I know. I know what you did for Mitchell. That you worked a deal for him."

"He's going to have to serve some more time."

"But he'll get out before the end of his sentence. And more importantly, you got him to do the right thing and get some other criminals off the street. You made him a hero again. You did that for me."

"And Jason."

While she'd been thrilled about her brother, she was more grateful to learn that Mitchell wasn't going to take Jason away from her—he'd already assured her of that. The little boy would legally become her son, very soon.

Kent's eyes narrowed as he studied her. "Are you mad about that?"

"I'm mad that you didn't tell me about Mitchell. Or about the surgery." Her breath caught. "I can't handle any more secrets, or people keeping things from me to protect me."

"Or themselves," he said, recalling her accusation.

"I want the truth from now on."

"I would never lie to you."

"I know that," she said, "but I want more."

"No more secrets. I will never keep anything from you again, Erin." He nodded with sudden understanding. "And I know what marriage means—sharing. *Everything*."

She smiled. "That's what it means to me, too."

"So will you marry me, Erin Powell? Will you and Jason become my family?"

"Yes!" a young voice shouted, as the little boy ran into the room.

"I'm sorry," Jason's grandmother said, her hair mussed as she hurried in after her grandson. "We didn't mean to intrude."

Erin smiled at her mother and then at her father, who walked in behind her. "I'm glad you're all here," she said. "Mom, you've already met Kent, but Dad, this is Sergeant Kent Terlecki."

Kent held out a hand to her father. "Nice to meet you, sir."

Her father shook it in both of his and swallowed hard. He was a man who respected hard work and integrity. "It's an honor, son."

It was right that her whole family—or at least most of her family—was there when she accepted the proposal of their newest member. Because of Kent, Mitchell would join them again, sooner than they'd expected.

Jason climbed into the bed with Kent and threw an arm across him in an exuberant hug. Erin winced and watched for Kent's grimace, but it never came. His only expression was one of love as he hugged her nephew back. "Hey, little buddy."

Kent gazed at Erin over the boy's head. "You haven't answered me yet," he stated.

"Yes!"

AFTER A ROUND OF congratulations, her parents took Jason down to the cafeteria. "There's something I haven't told you yet," Erin admitted.

"No more secrets," Kent reminded her.

"No more," she agreed. "Your parents are on their way to Lakewood."

He blinked as if confused, but his eyes were bright with hope. "My parents?"

"I sent them the most recent edition of the *Lakewood Chronicle.*"

"The one with your column about me?"

She nodded. "They called the chief. They're so sorry for shutting you out, Kent."

He expelled a ragged sigh. "I shut them out, too. Like I tried to shut you out, but you wouldn't let me."

"I knew you'd come around," she said as she took Jason's place, crawling into bed to lie beside him.

He wrapped his arm tightly around her shoulders. "You knew I'd propose?"

"Yes, but it took you long enough to ask me," she admonished.

Her fiancé grinned. "I had to get over that one little obstacle."

"The surgery?" she asked.

"No," he said, then chuckled. "Your hating my guts."

"Oh, that…" She couldn't remember now not loving him.

"Yeah, that." He brushed a kiss across her mouth.

"Down, boy." She pulled away as he deepened the kiss. "We don't want to rush your recovery."

"You're just worried that your parents will walk in on something else when they bring Jason back up," he teased. "They seem to be getting used to being grandparents."

She nodded with pride. Even her father, who'd been so disapproving of Mitchell's life choices, had fallen for the little boy. "Yes."

"Then they won't mind when we have kids."

"You have plans?" she asked.

Kent's gray eyes glowed with happiness. "For the past three years I didn't dare make plans because I didn't know what kind of future I'd have."

"And now?"

"Now I know that it'll be happy."

"Because the bullet's gone?"

He shook his head. "Because you're in my life. No matter what happens, we'll deal with it together."

That last niggling doubt, that he might push her away again if something bad happened, disappeared. She sighed and rested her cheek against his chest. "You're my hero."

"Not anymore," he scoffed.

"Once a hero..." Always *her* hero.

* * * * *

Watch for Lisa Childs's next book in the
CITIZEN'S POLICE ACADEMY *miniseries,*
ONCE A COP, coming September 2009,
only from Harlequin American Romance!

In honor of our 60th anniversary,
Harlequin® American Romance® is celebrating by featuring an all-American male each month, all year long with
MEN MADE IN AMERICA!
This June, we'll be featuring American men living in the West.

Here's a sneak preview of
THE CHIEF RANGER by Rebecca Winters.

Chief Ranger Vance Rossiter has to confront the sister of a man who died while under Vance's watch... and also confront his attraction to her.

"Chief Ranger Rossiter?" The sight of the woman who'd stepped inside Vance's office brought him to his feet. "I'm Rachel Darrow. Your secretary said I should come right in."

"Please," he said, walking around his desk to shake her hand. At a glance he estimated she was in her mid-twenties. Her feminine curves did wonders for the pale blue T-shirt and jeans she was wearing. "Ranger Jarvis informed me there's a young boy with you."

The unfriendly expression in her beautiful green eyes caught him off guard. "Yes," was her clipped reply. "When we arrived in Yosemite, the ranger told me I couldn't go anywhere in the park until I talked to you first."

"That's right."

"Knowing you wanted this meeting to be private, he offered to show my nephew around Headquarters."

So this woman was the victim's sister… "What's his name?"

"Nicky."

The boy who haunted Vance's dreams now had a name. "How old is he?"

"He turned six three weeks ago. Were you the man in charge when my brother and sister-in-law were killed?"

"Yes. To tell you I'm sorry for what happened couldn't begin to convey my feelings."

The woman's gaze didn't flicker. "I won't even try to describe mine. Just tell me one thing. Was their accident preventable?"

"Yes," he answered without hesitation.

"In other words, the people working under you fell asleep on your watch and two lives were snuffed out as a result."

Hearing it put like that, he had to set the record straight. "My staff had nothing to do with it. I, myself, could have prevented the loss of life."

Ms. Darrow's expression hardened. "So you admit culpability."

"Yes. I take full blame."

A look of pain crossed over her features. "You can just stand there and admit it?" Her cry echoed that of his own tortured soul.

"Yes." He sucked in his breath.

"I work for a cruise line. Aboard ship, it's the captain's responsibility to maintain rigid safety regulations. If a disaster like that had happened while he was in charge, he would have been relieved of his command and never given another ship again."

Rachel Darrow couldn't know she was preaching to the converted. "If you've come to the park with the intention of bringing a lawsuit against me for negligence, maybe you should." It would only be what he deserved.

"Maybe I will."

In the next instant, she wheeled around and hurried

out of his office. Vance could go after her, but it would cause a scene, something he was loath to do for a variety of reasons. In the first place, he needed to cool down before he approached her again.

The discovery of the Darrows' frozen bodies had affected every ranger in the park. A little boy had been orphaned—a boy whose aunt was all he had left.

* * * * *

Will Rachel allow Vance to explain—
and will she let him into her heart?
Find out in
THE CHIEF RANGER
Available June 2009 from
Harlequin® American Romance®.

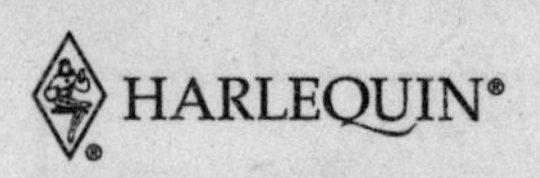

COMING NEXT MONTH

Available June 9, 2009

#1261 THE CHIEF RANGER by Rebecca Winters

Men Made in America

As the chief ranger of Yosemite National Park, Vance Rossiter isn't surprised to be confronted by Rachel Darrow, a woman whose brother perished on El Capitan during a blizzard. It happened on his watch, he's to blame—and he'll do anything to make things right. Including taking Nicky, Rachel's orphaned nephew, under his wing. And educating Rachel about what really happened that fateful day…

#1262 MOMMY FOR HIRE by Cathy Gillen Thacker

Why Grady McCabe needs to buy a wife is a mystery to Alexis Graham. The attractive and wealthy developer isn't looking for love—only a mother for his little girl. Alexis can't imagine marrying for anything *but* love. Then when the matchmaking widow tries to change a certain Texan's mind, he starts to relent… and fall for *her!*

A special, bonus story from The McCabes of Texas miniseries!

#1263 THE TEXAS TWINS by Tina Leonard

When New York billionaire John Carruth came to No Chance, Texas, to save their rodeo from bankruptcy, he had no idea he'd be meeting his twin brother. Jake Fitzgerald, champion bull rider, didn't know he had another half. John may be kin, but he's still a stranger in these parts. It's a showdown between two rivals, to see which brother will win the woman of his dreams—and be the town's savior!

The Billionaire *and* The Bull Rider—*2 stories in 1!*

#1264 WAITING FOR BABY by Cathy McDavid

Baby To Be

Lilly Russo is thrilled—and terrified—to be pregnant. It's a bit of a shock that her brief affair with the owner of Bear Creek Ranch, Jake Tucker, led to a new life growing inside her. She's worried about being a mom, but she's even more concerned about Jake, already a busy single father of three girls. Can their relationship grow from a fling into love—considering there's a baby at stake?